TAKEN FROM THE SEA

Colleen Monroe's Story

Cook's Cove

JUDY LESLIE

Judy Leslie

Copyright © 2024 by Judy Leslie

All rights reserved.

No part of this book may be reproduced in any form or by any electronic or mechanical means, including information storage and retrieval systems, without written permission from the author, except for the use of brief quotations in a book review.

ISBN: 979-8-9890819-7-4

Cover by: Covered by Melinda

https://www.coveredbymelinda.com

Also by Judy Leslie

Cook's Cove Women's Fiction Mysteries

The House at the Cove - #1 of duet

No Place to Hide - #2 of duet

Related Stand-alones

Strokes of Desperation

Taken From The Sea

The Shadows from the Past

Women's Fiction Small Town Romances

The Love in Leavenworth, WA Books Series

Renovating Hearts

Heart Strings

Rescuing You for Christmas

Love Among the Flames

Hearts Uncorked

Check out the release dates for Judy's upcoming books at www.judy-leslie.com

Contents

Taken From The Sea	vii
Prologue	1
Chapter 1	5
Chapter 2	10
Chapter 3	13
Chapter 4	26
Chapter 5	44
Chapter 6	51
Chapter 7	55
Chapter 8	62
Chapter 9	69
Chapter 10	75
Chapter 11	79
Chapter 12	88
Chapter 13	93
Chapter 14	102
Chapter 15	106
Chapter 16	112
Chapter 17	118
Chapter 18	128
Chapter 19	135
Chapter 20	142
Chapter 21	149
Chapter 22	156
Chapter 23	160
Chapter 24	173
Chapter 25	177
Chapter 26	182
Chapter 27	189
Chapter 28	196

Chapter 29	204
Chapter 30	212
Epilogue	219
Acknowledgments	221
About the Author	223

Taken From The Sea

COLLEEN MONROE'S STORY

A Cook's Cove
Mystery, Suspense, Romance

Prologue

Jason

The sound of the ocean's wildest roar causes angels to go scampering, running, hiding on the shore behind the evergreens, quivering down to their roots.

Looking out through the darkness, Jason MacGregor feels it in his bones. The monster of all storms is coming, and all the crab boats off the coast of Alaska will have to fight for their lives.

Recognizing the danger, the other fishermen, dressed in their waders, rain gear, and life jackets, busy themselves securing the traps on the deck. As the boat lifts higher and drops lower with each wave, Jason prays they are prepared, knowing death is breathing down his neck. In the distance, the sound of the serpent howls like an animal coming for its prey, snaking through the undulating sea toward them.

As the white caps push against their vessel, the boat leans to starboard, then to port. The wind whips waves across the bow, flooding the deck. Metal crab cages clank together, trying to break free. Spray stings the eyes of any man outside, blinding them to hope. All around him, men call out to God and those they love, hoping the lines they lash themselves to will hold while they ride the bucking sea. Shaking from fear and the cold, Jason grabs anything secure, trying to hang on long enough to make it inside without being swept away.

In an instant, a cable wraps around his ankle, and Jason is ripped from the deck and flung into the air like a flag on a pole. A swirl of confusion spins in his mind, and then a jolt of excruciating pain shoots through his leg. There, he hangs, upside down, from the arm of the crane. The constant pounding knocks the air from his lungs. Lightning lights up the sky, and his life flashes before him.

He's gone from boat to boat for the last twenty years, knowing his fate is intertwined with the sea. The unforgiving waters took his father when he was a teenager. Now, he may die here, as well.

Closing his eyes, he sees the gates of heaven swing open. Blinded by a radiant light, he's drawn toward a mirage. A woman draped in a seal coat stands before him, one foot planted on land, the other immersed in the shimmering water. Her long, dark hair cascades around her body, leaving him breathless. She's the most beautiful thing he's ever seen. He'd learned about selkies in a book he brought aboard just days ago. Now, one is extending her hand to him.

Suddenly, the pain filters through, jolting him back to reality. He pries his eyes open, only to discover he is lying on his side in a cramped bunk. The vision of the selkie woman is fresh in his mind. His lungs ache; the throbbing is excruciating. He coughs. A man touches his shoulder.

"Jason's returned from the dead!"

"I'm alive?" Jason tries to sit up, but pain shoots down his leg, and the room begins to spin.

"Patrick wasn't so lucky. He got swept away after getting you down from where you hung. Tom here managed to pull you inside the cabin before both of you ended up in the sea," Brian tells him.

Tom, an experienced old crabber, grunts without meeting Jason's eyes. "His leg is broken, and now that we know he made it, I guess we better try to put a splint around it."

Brian pats Jason's shoulder. "Someone get him a bottle of whisky from the cabinet to ease his pain. We're days from shore, and with the damage we've sustained, getting you to a proper doctor may take a bit longer."

Jason grits his teeth. He can see the blood-filled gauze around his leg and the point of the protruding bone where it pierced the skin. That is the price Neptune charged him for taking the sea's bounty. Looking up at the weather-beaten faces of the other fishermen surrounding him, his mind fills with remorse. The sea should have taken *him*, not Patrick. The man has a wife and family waiting for him back home. Jason knows no other life—no family, no children, no wife. Hell, he's never even been in love.

Jason tries to move his damaged leg, but the pain causes him to wince. He takes the whiskey that's offered and swallows a fair amount down. Wiping his mustache with the back of his hand, he sets his head down while they work on his leg.

They don't tell him, but he knows. He won't be able to return to the wilderness of these frigid waters and work alongside the other crabbers. He needs to find another way to live. Another place to live. Another life to live.

But the selkie woman from his dream is fresh in his mind, and he vows he'll find her someday.

Chapter One

Colleen

Colleen steps out of the water and tucks a beach towel around her damp body. Trotting barefoot through the warm sand, she hears her mother scream.

Colleen flies up the stairs at the back of their beach house to see what's the matter. Slumping in a wooden deck chair is her father. Next to him is a folded newspaper on the table beside a coffee mug. Her adoptive mother, Alice, is frantically shaking him.

"Dad!" Colleen races over. Her father's skin is pale. She presses her fingers to his neck, feeling for a pulse. Nothing. One minute passes, then two.

Colleen runs inside and grabs her cell phone from the kitchen counter. Fingers fumbling, she punches in 911. As she relays the emergency and rattles off their location to the dispatcher, she looks over at her dad's motionless body.

Medics arrive fifteen minutes later. As they work on her father's limp form, she knows in her heart it's already too late.

The shock is overwhelming. Hugging her mother tightly, Coleen wonders how his life could end like this. He appeared perfectly healthy this morning when they sat down for breakfast. What happened in the few short hours since that time?

After failing to resuscitate her father, one medic looks over and shakes his head, confirming her father is dead. Crying hysterically, her mother tears herself from Colleen's grip as the medics transfer her father's body onto a gurney. Muffling her cries with her palm, Colleen watches as they carry him away in the ambulance.

Looking down, a crumpled piece of paper skids across the deck toward her, stopping at her feet. Wiping her tears, she picks the paper up and takes it inside, smoothing it out on the counter.

Spare your family and relinquish control now before it's too late.

She bites her lip as she reads the ominous words. What do they mean? The note seems like a vague threat. She can't imagine who would want to threaten her father or family. He's a well-respected business owner.

Colleen read over the cryptic words again. Spare her family from what? And relinquish control of the business to who? None of it makes any sense. Crumpling up the paper again, she tosses it in the garbage, where it belongs.

SHE FEELS out of place at the funeral. Most of the mourners are people she doesn't know. They are her father's friends and people through work. Some businessmen from China even flew over to show their respect.

Thank God her friend Eric is here to lean on. He tucks his arm around her side as her tears flow. She is a fish out of water and desperately wants to run away and hide to mourn alone.

The day after the funeral, while her mother is sleeping off a Xanax, Colleen heads back to their beach cottage in Cook's Cove. Staying with her mother is draining, and she needs to get away. Her life is about to change. All of their lives are going to change.

Once she arrives at their ocean retreat, she takes a deep breath, unlocks the door, and then turns off the alarm. An eerie quiet greets her. The place is a single-level wood-framed house built by her grandparents to blend in with the tall evergreen trees. In the back, there's a large, expansive deck where they spend many hours barbecuing meals. A stairway leads to a private beach below.

Years ago, her mother replaced the formal furniture with denim chairs and a leather couch. The polished wood dining table is from a local woodworker. The paintings on the wall are all by a local artist who owns a gallery in town. Nothing in the house looks pretentious. It's their getaway house, not a showplace. Her father insisted they come here to live like a regular family instead of one of privilege. There are no servants to wait on them, like in her parent's home in Seattle. At this house, they hung up their wealth on the hook by the door when entering and traded their expensive shoes for sandals and flip-flops. Now, they could be an ordinary family enjoying the solitude of the beach.

A headache is now pounding in her head, so she trots over to her parents' bathroom for an aspirin. When she opens the cupboard, her father's pill bottles are lined up in a row. She has no idea what they are for and debates throwing them away. Her mother won't be able to deal with all her father's items here at the beach house, and soon, someone will arrive to clean everything out. On her next visit here, all his personal items will be gone like he never existed, leaving a big hole in their lives. Grabbing the aspirin, she leaves the drugs for the cleaners so they can properly dispose of them.

Next, she heads into the kitchen. Memories of that day flood back when she sees the chair on the porch through the window. Something's bugging her. She digs through the kitchen trash, fishing out the note she tossed. She reads it again and again, hoping some detail will reveal itself.

Colleen thinks back over the last few weeks before her dad's death, searching her memory for any indication of trouble. Lately, he seemed preoccupied, often staring off into space when they spoke, probably from the stress of work. He recently sold some business shares to Mr. Lei, the Chinese man who handles all the accounts from China. Which she knew he didn't want to do. The majority he kept for the family, though.

She taps the side of her mouth, wondering. Was her father worried about money? She should've asked more questions. Not that he'd share any information with her. Besides, she hates to admit it, but she has no idea what goes on at his office. It's like a computer game she doesn't know how to play.

She'll need more information to get to the bottom of this mystery. Crumpling the note, she shoves it in her pocket and goes to her father's home office. If there are any clues to be found, they'll be among his papers.

The office is meticulously organized, with files labeled in her father's neat handwriting. She opens drawers, rifling through folders. It's mostly just regular paperwork—financial statements, legal contracts—nothing suspicious.

Her eyes go to the bottom drawer of the heavy wooden desk. She tugs the handle, but it doesn't budge. *Duh.* Of course, her father kept it locked. Why did she expect it to open now?

Colleen grabs a paper clip from the desk, unbending it. She's picked a lock or two in her reckless youth and hopes she still has the knack. After a few minutes of jimmying the paper clip around, the lock clicks open. Holding her breath, Colleen pulls the drawer open.

Chapter Two

Colleen

There isn't much inside—a few old photos, her mother's jewelry case full of precious stones, and more legal documents. She is about to slide it closed when she notices a small thumb drive taped to the inside of the drawer. Carefully removing it, she plugs the drive into the computer.

A window pops open, showing a single encrypted file. Colleen's pulse quickens. She is no hacker, but she's seen enough movies to know encrypted files are for hiding secrets. What was her father hiding?

Opening a decryption program, she gets to work cracking the password. It takes almost half an hour of trying different combinations. She strikes gold when she types in "Flipper," her childhood nickname only her parents called her. Inside were several files, all similarly encrypted. Damn, she is not a computer nerd. It is going to take time to figure this out.

She glances out the window; the sun is sinking low over the ocean. She sighs, slipping the thumb drive into her purse to go through later. Next, she looks around to make sure everything's perfect. She doesn't want her mother to know she was snooping.

THE FOLLOWING DAY, Colleen finds herself empty without her father's presence. Grief clings to her, crushing her heart. He loved the ocean almost as much as she did, encouraging her to explore its mysteries.

Pacing along the shore, Colleen stops and sits on a washed-up tree. Stretching her feet out, wiggling her toes, her webs spread like wings. Reaching down and dusting the sand from her skin, she smiles at her unusual feet. She was born with syndactyly, a minor birth defect connecting her toes.

Her father encouraged her to keep her webs. When anyone was critical, he'd tell her not to listen to them and to follow her own path instead. So, with his support, she flaunted her uniqueness, never crumbling under the teasing of others. As a child, her sister, Jody, called her Duck Feet, but that never fazed her. Whenever her mother brought up getting the webs removed, her father would say, "It's Colleen's choice. She'll deal with it when she's ready."

Everyone thought Colleen would change her mind someday, but that never happened.

Colleen glances at the water. She misses her father—his

curly gray hair, deep voice, and the expression lines carved into his face from years of running his business.

She sniffs, remembering sitting in his arms as he told her tales of the places he'd been in his youth and how his grandfather started the Monroe Shipping business, hauling freight to Alaska and then the Orient—Japan, Thailand, and China. She could imagine traveling across the open water to other places, not on a large vessel, but on a sailboat —her sailboat.

Her lips tremble. She not only lost her father but also the dream of living the life she imagined for herself. He told her that someday this would happen. But she never thought it would happen so soon. Maybe ten years from now. But not now.

While he encouraged her to follow her dreams, Father also told her, "Monroe shipping plays an essential role in life. It keeps the world operating by delivering supplies to those who need them. Like the clothes you wear and the food you eat. Someday, you'll sit at the helm alongside your mother and Jody when I'm gone. The world will be waiting for the goods you'll send them."

Soon, the harsh reality that it's their responsibility to run the company now will change all their lives.

With a sigh, she says goodbye to the soothing presence of the ocean and heads back to her condo in Seattle.

Chapter Three

Colleen

Colleen digs through her clothes in her bedroom until she finds a suitable outfit: a navy pencil skirt, a white tailored blouse, and a light-blue sweater. She does a double-take in the mirror and rolls her eyes. This is something her mother would wear. Frowning, she mutters, "At least I'll fit in."

Passing on heels, she instead slips on extra-wide sneakers. Next, she smooths out her skirt, pulls her straight hair back in a silver clip, sprays the sides so they stay in place, then lets out a breath and leaves.

She shoves a stick of gum in her mouth and stares up at the forty-six-floor building. It towers above the others like a concrete-and-glass monument of success. The day-to-day operations of this business are foreign to her. Jody, her older sister, seems to be the only family member who genuinely shows interest in what happens at the office. Her mother hasn't been active in Monroe Shipping in years. Still, they are expected to fulfill her father's wishes to keep the business and maintain control. It's her family's legacy.

She takes the elevator to the top. The receptionist nods as Colleen strolls past, heading down the hall to her father's old office.

Opening the door brings back memories of her childhood. She recalls standing by the windows, looking at the city with her father. This is a corner office where you can see the vast water of Puget Sound. Container ships dot the horizon, waiting to dock like specks of coffee grounds in the bottom of a cup. Along one side is the wharf where ships unload goods from around the world. Way off in the distance to the south is Mt. Rainer. On a clear day, the mountain looks like a dish of vanilla ice cream.

"Well, I didn't expect to see you here," her sister Jody says, closing the door behind her, then walking over and sitting in their father's chair behind his desk.

"It's a little early to claim his office, don't you think?" Colleen replies, turning from the view to face her sister. Jody considers herself the poster child for women reaching for the golden ring of corporate success. However, being the boss's daughter, she took a shortcut, bypassing the more deserving by claiming her birthright. Deck out in her 'take me seriously' dark blue skirt and blazer with her blond hair tucked into a bun in the back of her head. It's obvious she's ready to claim her new role.

"What do you care? You've shown no interest in this place. It's mine now."

"I'm here, aren't I?" Colleen chews her gum, letting out a loud pop.

Jody swings the chair left and right with her foot. "Well, I guess you are. But I don't know what you can contribute."

"I'll not be some flunky file clerk. I have a degree in marine biology, you know."

"Please." Her sister rolls her eyes. "There aren't any positions open for a marine biologist here."

"I have just as much right to be here as you do," Colleen points out.

"Is that what you think? I earned this office while you were off playing. I know what goes on here, which is more than I can say for you. Besides, you could've shown some interest years ago if you wanted to work in Father's business."

"I'm willing to learn."

Jody waves a dismissive hand. "Well, as long as you're here, I'll send Betty over to give you something not too hard to do."

Colleen leaves, chomping her gum to relieve her stress. She'd have to prove to everyone that she isn't the spoiled child they think she is.

She daydreams about being out on the water while waiting in an empty office where a computer sits. When Betty enters, Colleen slips the gum out of her mouth and tosses it into the garbage.

Betty opens a program on the computer, showing Colleen what to do.

Swell, she'll be looking at dots on a screen representing boats arriving to be unloaded.

After an hour, her eyes blur. She fidgets, crossing and recrossing her legs. Her skirt is too tight, her blouse too stiff, and her mind keeps wandering. She wants to be out on the water—to feel the wind in her hair. Finally, she can't stand it and gets up, tells Betty she has an appointment, and leaves.

At home, she pulls out a carton of chocolate ice cream and a spoon. She begins eating away her anxiety, chastising herself for not making it for more than a few hours.

"I'm sorry, Daddy," she mumbles to a photograph of him on the wall while she licks the spoon. "Next time, I'll try to find something less boring I can do."

She remembers the flash drive she found at their beach house and starts up her computer. She shoves the last bite of ice cream in her mouth and hastily plugs the flash drive into the laptop. After using the password to open the file, she's surprised the others open up with the same code.

She skims through them - bank statements, legal contracts, photos. Most seem innocuous until a business contract catches her eye. Her dad's shipping company name is there, dealing with a Chinese manufacturer for a massive amount of money. The contract is dated just weeks before his death.

She digs deeper into the drive. More China connections emerge - a wire transfer to the company, restaurant expenses in Shanghai, hotel stays in Beijing, her dad posing with Chinese businessmen at a factory.

He was gone on a trip recently, but why is this information encrypted on the hard drive? Why keep this information a secret? Certainly, there are records at the office pertaining to any travel expenses. Perhaps it's a duplicate, but that doesn't make sense.

She bites her lip. This would make sense if she knew more about their shipping business.

"This is useless," she mutters, slamming the laptop

closed. None of it seems related to the mysterious note she found.

Getting up, she dumps the empty ice cream carton in the garbage and then changes into her sailing clothes. It's almost time for her class to begin. Locking the door, a sense of guilt sweeps around her. She owes it to her father to work at his company. She'll have to try harder.

OUTSIDE, her students are lining up, waiting on the dock for her. "I hope you've read your lesson so we can try out what you've learned," she cheerfully announces, helping the students aboard and pointing out their positions. She enjoys guiding new sailors in learning how to sail and navigate with the wind.

"The wind is not a constant mass coming from one direction. There's everything from puffs and spurts to breezes and steady winds. We can't use a computer to tell us everything, so you'll need to know how to read the water." She points out where to look for the wind, how to tack, which sail to choose to catch the breeze, and how to furrow a sail.

When they return to the dock, Colleen sees the smiles on their faces as they depart. It makes her happy to see them so pleased with their lessons. It's hard to explain the magic of it to people who spent their lives inside. You have to experience it—the freedom of gliding across the surface in the breeze, watching schools of fish beneath, orcas leaping into the air nearby, while seagulls soar overhead. To her, this is the essence of what life is supposed to be—not sitting behind a desk somewhere in a box.

Thank goodness it's Friday. After returning home, she packs her bag and leaves. Desperate to escape the city and all its distractions, Colleen drives to Cook's Cove.

OPENING THE DOOR, her mother's voice calls out to her, "Hello."

Colleen's brows knit together, and a frown forms on her face. Her mother is here. She must have parked in the garage, or a blue Lexus would be out front.

"What are you doing here, darling? I thought you would still be at the office in Seattle." Her mother's voice is dripping with disapproval.

Opening the refrigerator, Colleen pulls out a bottle of wine. Pouring herself a glass. She settles in a chair in the living room across from her mother. "Daddy's office feels so strange without him there. I don't have a clue what to do," she confesses.

"Jody's settled right in. Maybe you need to take on a more active role. Ask people for their help. I'm sure someone can show you what to do."

Taking a deep breath, Colleen set her glass on the side table, summoning her courage before asking, even though she already knows the answer. "Mother, I'd like to sail around the world," she says hesitantly. "Take a couple of years off. I could go to work at the shipping company when I get back."

Her mother's eyes flash with anger. "You'll do no such thing!"

Colleen slumps in her chair and pouts. "Why do you

dismiss it whenever I want to do something exciting?" She's frustrated. "I'm twenty-four and want to have an adventure before settling down. I want to sail to different places besides the water around here."

Unmoved by Colleen's outburst, her mother brings her glass to her lips, takes a slow sip, and replies, "I'm sure you can find something else to do that doesn't require a boat."

Pissed, Colleen crosses her arms in front of her. "You just don't understand. When father was alive, he encouraged me to try new things."

Her mother's face hardens. "Your father may have talked about adventures, but he followed the same path as his father did. Monroe Shipping is a family business. And like it or not, you'll carry on that legacy."

It's pointless to argue with her mother. Dreams of sailing away on a grand adventure are slipping further away each day.

They lapse into a long silence, avoiding conversation. Once the sun sets and dinner is over, Colleen goes to her room, picks up a book, and starts reading to forget about her problems.

Later that night, Colleen slips out of the house and goes to the beach. Above, the moon's face appears etched with graphite, and the stars poke holes in their nighttime blanket. The place is full of moonlight and shadows.

She walks along the water's edge as tiny bubbles gurgle between the rocks. A breeze ruffles her long hair, so she zips up her quilted puff coat to keep out the night's chill. A large bleached-out tree sits across the sand; it's been there for years. Snarled ribbons of seaweed cling to the tree's roots. Colleen sits down on the wood in the same place since childhood, adjusting her body to the familiar crack in the worn surface.

Off in the distance, a pinprick of light flickers from a fishing boat like a misplaced star. The water's vast, dark surface gives the illusion you could run across it, like a puddle on the sand, instead of a deep ocean of mystery.

Her ears catch a sound in the wind. She began hearing it at night out on the water just before her father died. It stirs a longing for love in her. Perhaps it's wishful thinking on her part—finding someone in the mist who truly understood *her* and could fill the emptiness she hides deep inside.

A beam of light bounces around, scanning the area, then lands on her. It's her mother notifying her that her private time is up and she needs to come inside. Colleen climbs off the log and walks back to the stairs. After a few steps, she let out a sigh. A heaviness replaces the carefree moment she found on the beach.

Colleen dusts off her webbed feet on the back deck, opens the door, and walks inside. She passes a body in the dark without saying a word, knowing it's her mother by the odor of smoke that always lingers around her. Colleen slips into her room, removes her coat, and climbs back into bed. There, she closes her eyes, picturing waves crashing against the shore. Eventually, the gentle rhythm lulls her to sleep.

COLLEEN PULLS out a chair from the table and sits down. She reaches for a banana, peels it open, and takes a bite as her mother's words jab at her.

"You're not a child anymore." Her mother lights a cigarette with a match, waving out the flame. "You need to grow up. Act as if you belong in this family instead of spending days in the water like a damn fish."

Colleen raises an eyebrow. "Belong in this family?" Though she is aware of her adoption, the subject is always shrouded in secrecy. Her inquiries about her birth mother are always met with icy stares, leaving her with more questions than answers. "What's that supposed to mean?"

Her mother exhales a cloud of smoke. "I think it's time you focus on the future. Other women your age follow their career paths, find husbands, and start families." A cough escapes her mother's lips, and she reaches for a napkin to dab at her mouth.

Colleen's frustration bubbles to the surface. "I'm not like other women. Besides, I *have* a job—teaching sailing and scuba diving."

"Oh, please." Her mother scoffs. "You need to give up that childish hobby. I expect you to work in the office regularly, not just whenever it suits your fancy."

Colleen fights the urge to roll her eyes. Now that her father isn't around to run interference, her mother is constantly nagging her.

Her mother stands across the table with a coffee mug in one hand and a perpetual stick of burning tobacco in the other. "You've spent too much time at this house." She lets out a puff of blue smoke. "I don't want you to come here until you've proven you can act like a responsible adult. You need to focus on your life in Seattle, not here playing in the water."

Angry, Colleen blurts, "I've come here my entire life.

You can't stop me. I have my sailboat moored at the marina in Cook's Cove, and it's all tricked out now for the long cruises I'm planning on taking in the future."

Her mother slams her coffee on the table, spilling the liquid on the placemat. "I want you out of here. Pack your things and go. I'll deal with you back in Seattle."

Hurt by her mother's rejection, Colleen stands, tossing her chair so it hits the ground with a bang. Stomping back to her room, she slams the door behind her. Why can't her mother understand? She is doing her best. She isn't like her sister Jody.

Colleen throws her clothes back into her suitcase. She's leaving for now, but plans to return when her mother isn't around to spy on her.

Making her way through the house, she stops at her parents' bedroom entrance to let her mother know she is leaving. The door's ajar. Pushing it open, she finds her mother leaning against the dresser, stroking a piece of fur, holding it to her chest, murmuring to it.

Colleen clears her throat. Her mother's eyes widen in surprise. Then she opens a drawer, slipping the fur inside, and closes it.

"I'm taking off now," Colleen announces, curious about what her mother was doing.

Alice nods without a word.

Shaking her head, Colleen leaves the room, picks up her suitcase, and goes outside, where a cool breeze is blowing. She sits behind the steering wheel of her red Mazda for a moment before starting the engine and heading toward downtown Cook's Cove. She isn't ready to leave just yet. As her foot presses on the accelerator, she is determined to figure out how to charter her own course.

AS COLLEEN STEPS into Joe's Coffee Shop, she recognizes her friend Jenny.

"Hi Colleen," Jenny's cheerful voice greets her. "It's been a while since we've seen you in town. How are you? You remember Vicki, right?"

Colleen's gaze shifts to Vicki, who appears holding two steaming cups of coffee. "Of course." Vicki nods in agreement.

"We have several of your paintings hanging in the living room of our beach house. And I'm well, thank you," Colleen replies.

Once Colleen settles into a chair at the table, Jenny gently touches Colleen's hand. "Sorry to hear about your father. He was a nice man."

Colleen swallows back her grief, mustering a smile to mask the lingering pain. "Yes... I'm still not used to the fact that he's gone. It's turned our lives upside down."

"Is that why we never see you anymore?" Jenny asked.

Colleen's brows furrow and she sighs. "Apparently, I'm supposed to spend more time in Seattle and less here, according to Mother."

"Why?" Jenny inquires. "I thought you loved it here. "

"I think your boat looks great, by the way. Maybe you can take us out some time," Vicki comments, sipping her drink.

Colleen's lips curl into a smile at the mention of her boat. "Yes, that would be fun." She turns to Jenny, eager to shift the focus away from herself. "I understand you and Shaun are together now."

"Yes, can you believe it? Who'd have thought I'd find someone like him? He's such a sweetheart."

"What about you?" Vicki asks playfully. "Any hunks joining you on the water?"

Colleen laughs. "No, that's not likely to happen." She has a habit of frightening men once they realize how different she is.

Jenny reaches out, gently patting Colleen's arm. "You'll find someone. Just give it time."

Colleen leans back in her chair. "I'm not like either of you," she replies. "Finding a man who shares my love for the water isn't easy." She glances out at the cove.

"I'm sure he's out there somewhere, searching for you," Jenny offers.

"I wouldn't bet on it." Colleen's gaze returns to her friends. "Thanks. Well, I'd better go back to Seattle. I have someone who wants me to check out a boat he's looking to buy." Colleen stands up with her cup in hand.

"Anyone interesting?" Vicki asks.

"No, he's an old guy who already owns a boat. He's just thinking of getting a bigger one. I've been putting off helping him figure out what to get because I don't know how serious he is. Maybe it's just a dream he'll never fulfill." Sadness washes over her. "I better go."

Both women jump up and hug her.

"Call me when you plan on coming here again, and we can have a girls' night out," Jenny volunteers.

"That'd be nice." Colleen smiles and waves goodbye. She misses hanging out with her girlfriends in Cook's Cove.

Rather than taking the freeway, Colleen follows the coastal route to Seattle. While driving with the top down, thoughts fly through her head and get tangled in her mind.

Maybe she is acting like a brat. Her mother is getting old and acting strange—stranger than usual. The added responsibility of Father's shipping company has to be hard on her. *But why take it out on me? Maybe they should've picked another baby instead of me—one with the same dreams they had.*

Chapter Four

Colleen

Hurrying down the office hallway, Collen hears Jody's voice, so she turns to face her sister.

"I'm surprised to see you back here." Jody's judgmental tone hangs in the air.

Colleen shrugs. "I'm not working today. I'm just meeting Eric. We're going to lunch at the aquarium." She isn't ready to sit and stare at the dots again. They need to give her something less boring if they want her to work here.

Colleen watches as Jody's eyes scan her outfit from head to toe. She purposely chose what she's wearing to reflect her true self — black designer jeans and a T-shirt with the words *Screw it. I'd rather be sailing* embellished across the front in blue. Her nails are black, and her hair's in a braid down the back. She also inserted a gold hoop on the side of her nose. Why pretend she's someone she isn't?

Her sister's words are dripping with sarcasm. "Go play with the fish where you belong."

Colleen resists a snarky reply and heads for the door. She isn't going to let her sister's comments affect her day. Despite what others think, she's comfortable with herself.

Once she reaches Eric's office, she wraps her knuckles against the door and peeks inside. "You ready?" She smiles.

Eric glances up from his desk. He pushes his dark hair out of his eyes and gives her an intense gaze. "Yes, give me a minute. I need to make a quick phone call." He reaches for the phone. "I'll meet you downstairs in the lobby."

With the phone cradled against his shoulder, he shuffles his papers into a neat pile and slides them into a drawer, locking it.

Colleen nods, her smile widening as she walks away, reflecting on their relationship.

They'd met the year before when he started working for Monroe Shipping. Her father introduced them, and she was immediately curious about him.

Eric's jet-black hair hung over thick eyebrows. His piercing dark eyes were like polished stone, his nose prominent, not delicate at all. His handsome, exotic looks and international background intrigued her. There was a mysterious aura about him she found sexy.

Her father excused himself, leaving them alone to get to know each other. Eric's gaze locked on her. "You're gorgeous," he told her, his voice almost a whisper. "You're not at all what I expected."

"What were you expecting?"

"Definitely not someone as good looking as you."

She blushed, flattered yet nervous at the same time. Eric leaned in closer, his breath hot against her ear. "I'd like to get to know you," he whispered, stirring up a quandary of emotions in her.

She soon discovered beneath his facade of elegance was a man covered in tattoos with many interests.

He knew the best places to eat, treating her to authentic Chinese food where she tasted exotic dishes. The Jade Dragon was her favorite. The chef's specialty was a delicious fish dish that melted in her mouth and spices that left a hot tingle on her tongue.

After finishing their first meal at the restaurant, Eric leaned back in his chair. "In Hong Kong, there are many late-night dim sum eateries with customers eating plates of siu mai, chari, and fried noodles well into the early morning hours."

She could imagine the smell of fried dumplings and caramelized pork, fish, and red chilies cooked all day in clay pots and rice steamers.

Eric shared stories with her about growing up in Hong Kong, with all its flash and glory, the wild nightlife—a lifestyle she found strange and intimidating but was curious about.

He grinned at her. "You think you have a nightlife here? You have no idea what fun is."

Colleen raised her eyebrows. "Oh, really?" She wasn't one to go out at night. She knew nothing about what went on at the different clubs around town.

Eric sipped his drink and shared, "There are live music venues showcasing everything from Cantonese opera to indie rock bands."

It all sounded so exotic and foreign to her.

He leaned forward. "In Hong Kong, the parties start after midnight and keep going all night. Clubs are pumping, markets packed, and the streets pulsing with energy."

Colleen imagined the bright neon lights and crowds of people out enjoying the midnight hours.

Eric's words made her realize how sheltered her life was, motivating her to venture out and experience the world before it was too late. She had no intention of living vicariously through people's lives like Eric. She wanted to experience things for herself. Sailing around the world had always been her dream, not dancing 'til dawn.

Eric rattled on, "In the clubs' VIP sections, champagne bottles are free-flowing. Special guests even have private doors to avoid the lines. Inside, you sit on plush seats while scantily dressed hostesses serve you." He winked at her.

Colleen remembered blushing. "That sounds a bit much to me."

He grinned. "You say that now. But when the music moves you, and the lights dazzle..." His face held a wide grin as his voice trailed off.

"I don't know. I don't think I would enjoy that." She wasn't a party person.

"But isn't it fun to indulge sometimes? Try something completely different." He gave her a mischievous smile, took her hand, and squeezed it. "I could show you a night you'd never forget."

She wasn't sure what he meant by that.

After their first night in bed, in which he totally focused on her, she ran her finger along the scar on his left arm. "How did you get this?"

"I grew up in a tough neighborhood and got it in a knife fight when I was young."

"Were you in a gang?"

"You could say that." He put his finger to his lips like it was a secret.

As she traced the curves of his body, she could feel the subtle tension beneath his bare skin. "Is that when you got your tattoos?" Her eyes trailed down his back, where two ancient samurai warriors stood with their swords drawn in battle, then to the intertwined dragons that coiled around his right arm. His chest was covered in odd symbols and Chinese characters.

"I guess so. I don't remember."

"I only have one tattoo. I wish I could get more, but Mom would have a fit."

"I like your tattoo, even if it is just of a tiny fish." He got out of bed and slid his black silk pajama pants on.

"It's not a fish. It's a seal." It was discreetly placed on the left side of her belly button.

Placing her chin on her elbows, she watched him. He had a nice muscular body from doing martial arts. "What did your mother think about you being in a gang?"

Eric sat down next to her, reflecting for a moment. Then a smile tugged at the corners of his mouth. "She didn't like it. In fact, she kicked me out of the place where we lived, which was okay. It was a dump."

"Oh, that sucks." Coleen bit her lower lip. She couldn't imagine what his life had been like.

"Yes, but my uncle took me in and made me learn English and study business so that I could help him at work. I did well in school, and when I got older, I applied to colleges in the US. I got accepted at the University of Washington."

"You must be a pretty smart guy because now you're working for my dad's company."

He pushed her hair aside. "Yes, and I got to meet you." He leaned over and kissed her while pushing her back down on the bed and pulling off her socks.

"No!" Colleen protested. Now, he'll think she was some sort of freak.

"What are you afraid of?" He examined her foot. "Oh, cool, you've got weird feet." He tickled the bottom, and she giggled.

Soon, they were an item, and he introduced her to many new things. She watched Chinese movies with subtitles. They went to the art museum to see the Chinese exhibition, and he explained the cultural background of each piece.

"You know, if we were to get married, I would be a shoo-in for a higher-level position and could personally show you the highlights of Hong Kong." Eric teased her.

But she knew that would never happen. She had other plans for her life that didn't include the flashiness of Hong Kong. Besides, she doubted Eric Lau would like her world of being out on the water. She enjoyed being around Eric, but there was something about him she couldn't put her finger on. He was sometimes distant, and she wondered if the chemistry wasn't there for him anymore and if he was bored with her. She certainly couldn't compete with his wild experiences in Hong Kong. She found him intriguing, but he was not the man she wanted to spend the rest of her life with. They were better off as friends than lovers, and eventually, he agreed.

She looks up as Eric steps out of the elevator with his jacket tossed over one shoulder, interrupting her memories. He kisses her on the cheek. "How was your weekend in Cook's Cove?"

"Mother is losing it. I know I shouldn't say anything, but don't count on her getting involved in what goes on here."

"Your sister seems to have set herself up as the one in charge anyway," he chuckles. "Mr. Lei isn't too happy with that. They seem to butt heads a lot."

"Yes, Jody can be a pain in the ass. Mother is pressuring me to work here, too, but I think I'd only get in the way. Can you believe they gave me the task of tracking where boats are?" She rolled her eyes. "Talk about boring."

"It's just as well you don't want to get involved with the company."

"What do you mean?" she asks, only mildly curious.

He places his hand on her back, guiding her out the door. "Let's go. We can talk about it later."

They crawl into their Lyft to the Seattle Aquarium. Eric is silent during the ride, looking out the window as though deep in thought.

After they arrive, they join the line to purchase tickets at the entrance. In front of them is a young woman with a child eager to see the different fish, which makes Colleen smile. She glances around as they nudge forward and notices two men standing to the side.

Inside the building, Eric guides her to a corridor and suggests, "Since your father is gone, now is the perfect opportunity to follow your dreams and sail to Hawaii. It's what you've always wanted—to have a life away from here.

Why not sell your shares so you can be free from this place at last?"

Colleen frowns. "Unfortunately, I can't do that. I need to hold on to my shares out of respect for my father."

"I'm sure you'd get a fair price. Heck, you'd be a millionaire. Then you'd never have to worry about working in an office again," he answers with a smile that seems a little too wide.

"As much as I want to leave everything behind, I can't. Mother would kill me if I even mentioned selling my shares."

Eric glances back briefly. Curious, she peeks behind her. The same two men she noticed outside are watching her. One holds his hand to his ear as though listening to something through an earbud.

"I'm just concerned about your safety," he tells her.

She arches her eyebrows.

"Well, don't say I didn't warn you."

"Warn me?" Now she's worried. "Is there something you aren't telling me, Eric?"

"Just forget I even mentioned it. We should go inside." He ushers her along.

Upon entering the central dome, everything Eric told her before vanishes from her mind, and her face lights up. Some people enjoy walking through gardens with flowers in bloom; she enjoys walking through this marvelous place with many colors and shapes gliding overhead. It contains a calming effect, reminding her another world exists beneath the ocean's surface.

They wander around the room for a while as fish glide past, a parade of shapes and colors pushing the water with their fins and wiggling their bodies as they move gracefully like dancers, pivoting in unison at a moment's notice. Some travel by in schools, while others choose to be independent. Larger ones open and close their mouths, mumbling in a language of bubbles. It is an enchanting place, a place she never grows tired of.

Eric checks his watch. "Come on. We need to grab a bite at the snack shop. I have to get back to work soon."

"I could spend all day in this room," Colleen sighs.

He shakes his head, grinning. "Most people I know find places like this boring. But not you. You are one of a kind."

"I love the water. I like to get away on my boat whenever I'm stressed." She smiles, then slyly adds, "I have a secret place I sail to."

"Around here?" he asks, perking up.

"No, farther north. I keep my boat at the marina in Cook's Cove. I know of an island off the coast of Bellingham in Puget Sound. It's an animal sanctuary with a lot of seals. It's where I go to unwind."

He shakes his head, smirking. "You certainly are a water rat."

"I'm not a rat!" She punches his arm playfully.

After a quick bite and a drink, Colleen and Eric return to the outside world. The sun is peeking out from behind what appears to be the only cloud in the sky. They walk to the edge of the parking lot, but Eric continues down the street.

Colleen stops abruptly. "Shouldn't we call for a ride? Don't you need to hurry back?"

"It's such a nice day; I thought we could take the bus instead." He points to the sky.

"Sure. I haven't taken a bus in ages."

They chat as they stroll to the bus stop. "Thanks for the necklace. It's so beautiful. I think I'll never take it off."

"I thought you'd like it. I had it specially made for you. Are you wearing it now?" he asks.

"Of course." She shows it to him. It's an aqua-blue square with a seal embossed in the middle.

Eric smiles, then leans over and kisses her on the lips.

"I thought we were just friends now," she says, slightly confused by his action.

He pulls her into a hug. "You are so amazing. I just wanted to show you how much you mean to me."

"Oh." She blushes.

As they wait for the light to change at the street corner, Colleen is aware of someone standing behind them. She casually glances back to see the same two men in black suits she saw earlier near the aquarium. One has large, dark-framed glasses.

At that moment, the light changes, and Eric starts across the road. Colleen runs a couple of steps to keep up. Once they reach the other side, she catches Eric's sleeve between her fingers and tugs lightly to get his attention.

"Those men are making me uncomfortable. They've been behind us since we left the aquarium."

Eric looks over his shoulder. His eyebrows lift, and he frowns. He reaches over and takes Colleen's hand. They quicken their pace, darting around people meandering down the street. When Colleen glances back, she crashes into a woman who suddenly appears in her way.

While stopping to help the woman, her eyes shift. The Asian men are gaining distance behind them.

Eric looks back. "I think we should split up," he tells her. "They may be after me."

Her eyes widen. "Why? Are you in trouble?"

"I'll call you tonight." He squeezes her arm and takes off running. She stands there, trying to make sense of what he'd just said. The men fly by, chasing after him, almost knocking her over. The three of them disappear around the building on the corner.

A sick feeling creeps into her. Not knowing what else to do, she calls a Lyft to take her to her condo.

Once inside she notices the flash drive is missing from where she thought she left it earlier. Searching her purse to see if it's there, she comes up empty-handed.

Pacing the floor, her gut's telling her that Eric hasn't returned to the office. She calls his cell phone several times while staring out the window in her living room. But he doesn't pick up. Worried, she calls Jody.

"So, how was your date with Eric Lau?"

Colleen leans against the wall, gazing out the window, toying with the edge of the curtain. She doesn't know what's going on, but she has to tell someone.

"Jody, I found a strange note the day Dad died, and later a flash drive at the beach house containing a bunch of encrypted stuff. Today, Eric told me he's concerned about Father's business. He thinks something might happen if—"

"You stole Dad's flash drive from the house? That's why you called? It's probably just old insurance records. Just the same, you better give it back to Mom."

"I don't have it now. I can't find it. I think something is going on, and we need to do something."

"Are you making this up?"

"No, listen to me—"

"Why should I listen to you? You don't care about anyone but yourself. You don't deserve your share of

Father's business. You're not even related to us. So, keep your nose out of what goes on here."

She ignores her sister's jabs. "I think something happened to Eric. Some men were after him. I've tried calling him, but he's not answering."

"Maybe he's tired of you."

Colleen holds the end of her braided hair to her mouth and then drops it. "No, Jody, listen to me."

"I have better things to do than to listen to your wild stories."

The line goes dead. Colleen drops the phone from her ear and focuses on the expansive view beyond her window. The sunlight on Lake Union glitters back at her. What Eric said about selling her shares in her family's business concerns her, along with the note and missing hard drive. Did Eric know something he wasn't telling her, and why were those men chasing him?

She bites her thumbnail. *I hope you're some place safe, Eric.*

AFTER A NIGHT of watching National Geographic episodes about sea creatures, morning arrives with a sinking sense of worry gnawing at Colleen. Once again, she calls Eric's cell phone. But still gets no response. Having left countless voice messages already, she tries calling the office.

"Can I speak to Eric Lau?" she asks his assistant. "This is Colleen Monroe. It's important."

"I'm afraid he's not here. I got a message; he wouldn't be in today."

Colleen's brows furrow: confusion mingles with her growing unease. If this is true, why didn't he tell her he wouldn't be at work? Doubt creeps into her mind. Something is going on.

As the day progresses, she anxiously waits for his return call, clinging to a flicker of hope that he will reach out to her. But the phone remains silent.

Unable to bear the uncertainty any longer, Colleen drives to Eric's apartment.

She marches toward his door and pounds her knuckles on it. No one answers.

Glancing up and down the corridor, she raises her voice. "Eric, if you're in there, please open the door."

A heavy silence fills the hallway, amplifying her anxiety. She puts her head against the door and listens, but there is no sound of movement from inside. Her eyes dart from side to side. She jiggles the door handle, but it's locked.

Colleen's mind races with questions as an overwhelming sense of helplessness sweeps through her.

After five minutes, Colleen's impatience grows unbearable. She takes the elevator back downstairs to the lobby and approaches the concierge desk. "Could you let me into Eric Lau's apartment?" she desperately asks. "It's number eight sixteen. I want to see if he's okay. He hasn't been answering my calls." She rubs her hands together impatiently.

The woman glares at her, obviously annoyed by the request. "No, I'm afraid I can't do that. I don't have permission to let you in. If you're that worried about him, you should contact the police."

Colleen bites her thumbnail. Should she take the concierge's advice and contact the police? Would they even take her seriously, or would they dismiss her like her sister Jody did? She needs to find a way into Eric's apartment to be sure he is missing before going to the police.

The concierge's phone rings, and she turns away to answer it. "I'm sorry to hear that. I'll be right up." She hangs up the phone. "Excuse me." She pushes back from her desk.

Colleen watches as the woman gets into the elevator. As soon as the doors slide closed, Colleen slips behind the desk and starts opening drawers. In the fourth drawer, buried beneath a stack of papers, she finds a master key. With a glimmer of hope, she slips it into her pocket and heads up the stairs to avoid encountering the concierge in the elevator.

She's out of breath by the time she reaches the eighth floor. Shoving the heavy fire door open, she runs down the hall and puts the key in Eric's lock.

As Colleen steps into the dimly lit apartment, her eyes strain to adjust to the darkness.

Eric's Chinese art collection on the walls, painted in bright colors, looks muted in the shadows. The space lacks the usual sounds of music, laughter, and the smells of exotic foods on the stove. Instead, silence and emptiness fill the air.

Upon entering Eric's bedroom, Colleen finds the light switch and turns it on, illuminating the space with a soft glow. Her eyes scan the room. A large tapestry of intertwining dragons hangs above the bed. The furniture, while simple in design, exudes an understated elegance. Ornate wood lamps with carvings of vines cast light and shadow on the walls.

She shouldn't be snooping, but she can't help herself. She goes to the closet, opens the door, and peeks inside. A row of neatly hung shirts and pants are on one side, and a collection of silk pajamas and robes on the other. She closes the doors, scanning the room until her eyes fall on his black lacquer dresser. There sits a brass tray containing a single coin. Curious, Colleen walks over and picks it up, examining it. Embossed on the coin is a circle with a dragon in the middle. She remembers Eric liked to collect antiques from China. Wondering about its age and origin, she reaches for her phone and takes a picture.

The sound of the front door opening sends Colleen's heart racing. Her face flushes with relief and embarrassment—Eric's returned home, and she is snooping in his apartment.

She makes her way to the living room. To her surprise, instead of finding Eric, there is a man she's never met standing there. He's slender, with black hair gelled up into spikes. His dark eyes and long, black lashes peek out from under hooded lids. He's wearing slacks and a white T-shirt with dark Chinese characters on the front. She's hoping he's one of Eric's friends since he came barging in like that.

"What are you doing here?" the man asks curiously.

Caught off guard by this man's unexpected presence, the words tumble out of Colleen's mouth in a rush. "I was looking for Eric Lau," she confesses. "I... I was worried because he hadn't answered his phone or responded to the messages I'd left." Her fingers fidget nervously with the coin she's holding in her hand.

"Me too. I was hoping to find him here." He holds out his hand to shake. "I'm Lee Jun, a...friend of his."

Colleen relaxes a bit, setting the coin on the red lacquered tabletop next to them. "Colleen Monroe," she tells him, taking his hand.

"Eric told me about you." He smiles, then looks at what

she'd set on the table. "What's this?" He picks up the coin, bringing it close to his face.

Hesitant at first to tell him, she gives in and replies, "I found it on Eric's dresser. I shouldn't be snooping, but I was looking for clues that might explain his sudden disappearance."

Lee Jun lifts his eyes. "Do you know what this symbol means?" He glares at her.

"No," she admits.

He sets the coin back down. "It means trouble, and we should get the hell out of here right now."

Colleen is full of questions. However, Lee Jun vanishes through the door before she can ask him anything, leaving her alone in the apartment. A chill runs up her spine as Colleen glances around the space, suddenly unnerved by the shadows stretching between the furniture items. Leaving the coin on the table, she hurries out the door.

Colleen finds the concierge talking to two people at the desk in the lobby. Seizing the opportunity, she drops the master key to the floor when they aren't looking. Glancing over her shoulder, she slips out of the building.

Colleen heads for the coffee shop around the corner, where she orders tea. Hoping to soothe her nerves, she finds an empty table by the window. She pulls out her phone and opens the photo of the coin she found at Eric Lau's apartment. The sight of it alarmed Lee Jun. Curious, she searches for dragon designs on the internet. After scrolling through countless pages, she finds one that matches the image. It's a symbol for the Triad, a notorious Chinese crime syndicate. *Oh my God, were they the ones after Eric?*

Lost in her thoughts, Colleen gazes out the window, letting her eyes wander aimlessly as she exhales a deep breath. A car slowly rolls down the street. She stirs her tea, contemplating her next move. Now what? If she calls the police, they'll ask her questions she doesn't have answers for. Eric must have known something strange was going on, and now he is in trouble for trying to warn her. With a sense of urgency gnawing at her, against her better judgment, Colleen punches in the number for her sister.

"I'm busy, so make this short," Jody's voice snaps at her through the phone.

"Eric—"

Her sister's impatience is evident. "Colleen, I don't have time for your relationship problems right now. Deal with them yourself."

The phone line abruptly goes dead.

Damn it. Colleen blows out her breath. She needs Jody to listen to her. There's no one else to turn to. Certainly not their mother.

She opens her text messages attaching the photo of the coin she'd discovered in Eric's room to her text: **If Eric doesn't show up for work tomorrow, call the police and show them this.** She hits send, hoping her sister takes her seriously and takes action.

Colleen rises from her seat, pushes her chair in, and drops her cup in the garbage on the way out. Worry grows inside as she strolls back to where she left her car. Should she return home and wait?

Once she reaches the corner, she glances over her shoulder and tenses up. Her heart skips a beat as her eyes fall on a stocky man in a black suit half a block behind her.

Shit.

A surge of adrenaline courses through her veins. She takes off running for her car. On the way, she misses a step and stumbles to the ground. Pushing herself up, the man following her reaches out. Springing to her feet, she knees him in the balls and resumes running.

She jumps in behind the wheel of her car and peels out of the garage entrance, almost hitting another car on the street. At the light, a black vehicle pulls up behind her. In her rear-view mirror, she sees two men; one with dark-framed glasses. The same men who were following Eric outside the aquarium.

Colleen sits up straight, gripping the steering wheel with both hands. As the light changes, she presses her foot down hard, racing forward, then cranking the wheel left in front of an oncoming car, cutting between pedestrians crossing the street. The brakes squeal, but she keeps going, zigzagging through streets until she finds the entrance to the freeway.

Adrenaline flowing, she speeds up, cutting in and out of traffic. Scanning her mirrors for the black car, it seems she's lost them.

She doesn't allow herself to relax until she is out of town and the scenery around the freeway changes. She takes an off-ramp, traveling residential streets until she finds the coastal road leading to Cook's Cove, hoping they won't follow her here. Her tires screech to a halt at the marina, her heart pounding against her chest. *Breath*, she tells herself, choking in the air.

Chapter Five

Colleen

The sun drops, and the incoming tide now pushes at the dock. The salty scent of the sea mingles with the evening breeze as Colleen steps aboard Paradise, her Erin Citation thirty-four-foot sailboat. Undoing the ropes and pulling in the buoys, her body adjusts to the boat's movement. She makes her way to the stern and starts the engine. With steady hands on the wheel, she skillfully steers away from the marina. She guides Paradise westward through the cover of night, where she last saw the sun sink below the horizon. Glancing back, she spies the faint glow of headlights as a car pulls into the marina parking lot. *Did someone follow her there?*

With worry on her mind and troubles stalking her, the allure of the sea calls to Colleen. It's the only place she's free. The night's cool wind brushes her face as she stands at the wheel, steering the boat to her sacred place. Her ebony hair billows behind her like untamed strands of silk as the wind runs its fingers through it. Above her, the night sky twinkles with a tapestry of stars, and the face of the moon looks down upon her.

As she approaches the tiny island, ripples splash against the hull. She kills the engine and drops the anchor. Here, in this peaceful sanctuary, she hopes to remain hidden. Tonight, she'll sleep onboard her boat. At first light, she'll search for a place to hide.

Thoughts race through her mind as she contemplates her options. She could stop at one of the San Juan islands and get supplies, leave Puget Sound, head for the open sea, and sail down the coast to Oregon. After that, she could stock up and maybe head for Hawaii.

She frowns. As much as she wants to leave, running away from her life isn't the answer. Besides, she owes it to her father to return and participate in his business, even if her role is minor. Contacting the police is the best option. They can solve the mystery.

Colleen grabs a bottle of wine from the refrigerator and pulls out the cork, filling her glass. Looking up at the night sky, she stares into space. Soon, her body relaxes, and she lets go of her troubles.

Pouring another glass of wine, listening. In the distance, a strange sound travels in waves on the wind. It's a song, or at least she thinks it is. Her mind stirs. She's heard it before. However, she can't place where or when.

After she finishes her drink, she heads below deck to her bunk and crawls in. The gentle rhythm of the waves against the boat rocks her to sleep.

AT DAWN, seals climb onto the deck and nudge open the hatch. A low growl pulls her from sleep. They tug at her blanket, letting the cool air touch her skin. Colleen turns and then sits up. Big, dark eyes stare at her. They smell of the sea—salt and fish. The large creatures wiggle and use their flippers to go back upstairs.

Colleen climbs out of her bunk. Discarding her nightshirt, she pulls on her wetsuit and zips it up. Its gray, spotted design resembled the sleek skin of a seal, allowing her to mingle with these marvelous creatures underwater. On the deck, she tucks her hair securely inside the cap. The seals slip into the water one by one, their heads bobbing, watching as if calling for her to join them. Colleen adjusts her diving tank, pulls down her face mask, puts her legs over the side, the mouthpiece in, and jumps.

Beneath the waves, Colleen enjoys a sense of liberation from being one with the creatures that surround her. She follows their lead away from the boat to the nearby refuge island. Now, she's only a shadow in the water.

As she approaches the shallow pebbles below, she pushes toward the surface. Breaking free from the depth, she looks at the island. Spotting a secluded spot along the shore, she swims toward it. This is her secret place, where she escapes from all the stresses of the world. Here, she can be alone.

Emerging from the sea, she steps onto the sand, her feet sinking into the warm softness. She removes her face mask and sets her tank on the sand, leaving them at the water's edge. The rising sun casts a glow on the gray rocks where small groups of seals are resting. Their bark welcomes her. Walking farther up the beach, she removes her hood and shakes out her long hair, allowing it to cascade down her back, combing it with her fingers. She unzips the front of her suit and sheds it, discarding it on the sand. Without the confinement of clothing, she climbs to a flat, worn rock, sets her elbows on the hard surface behind her, and leans back, letting the sun caress her bare body.

The warmth feels good. Colleen pushes strands of her hair off her chest and flicks them over her shoulder. The surrounding seals shift, readjusting as they return to their spots, grunting at one another. Thin clouds traverse the sky overhead while gray seagulls ride the wind like kites in flight. Breathing in the salt-tinged air, she tastes the sea on her lips. The rhythmic lapping of the tide becomes her heartbeat, its ebb and flow resonating within her soul. At this moment, in this sliver of paradise, she's free from the expectations of her mother and sister and her thoughts about her father, Eric, and the men following her. All her worries and troubles dissipate in the gentle breeze, leaving a profound sense of peace within her. She closes her eyes.

Stretching her arms, the mood shifts around her, and a sudden commotion disrupts her tranquility. The seals, once calm, now grunt and bark, their bodies scattering across the rocks. Colleen's eyes snap open, her senses heightened by their confusion. In a split second, her instincts kick in, propelling her into action.

A woven net sails through the air, crossing her line of vision. *What the heck?* She rolls to the side, dodging it before it lands. Springing to her feet, adrenaline surges through her. Sensing her urgency, the seals circle her, forming a protective barrier.

A voice cuts through the barking chaos. "No, you don't. You ain't getting away from me!"

Alarmed, Colleen jumps from the rocks and runs toward the shore, where she left her scuba equipment. Fumbling with her wet suit, she pulls it up over her body, zips it closed, and tucks her hair in the cap.

From behind a boulder, a man charges toward her with his arms outstretched. As he reaches for her, she picks up a stick and swings it, smashing it against his face. He curses, and his hand goes up to the blood dripping from his nose.

Raising her foot, Colleen kicks him in the chest, sending him tumbling over the seals behind him. As he struggles to regain his balance, the seals move to create a wiggling obstacle course for him to maneuver around. Sprinting to the beach, she quickly fastens on her tank and breathing apparatus. She runs to the incoming tide and dives head first, slicing through the water with effortless grace.

With adrenaline flowing through her, Colleen propels herself through the murky depths, scattering schools of fish in her wake. Glancing at the light of the surface, she spots Paradise and heaves herself over the railing.

Onboard, she removes her mask and tank, letting them fall to the deck with a clatter. The chain of the necklace Eric gave her snaps. The delicate seal pendant bounces on the bow before slipping from her grasp, then plunges into the water below. She sighs, retrieving it is out of the question.

Shielding her eyes from the glaring sun, she scans her surroundings to see if any boats are nearby. She spots two: a sleek black cruising boat and a fishing boat. Not knowing if she is being pursued or which vessel holds the man who tried to capture her, she cranks up her anchor and runs to the back to start the engine. Her gut is telling her she is in danger, and she can't just sit out there and wait to find out why.

Gripping the wheel tightly, her only focus is to get the hell out of there. The wind whips through her hair, and the ocean spray mists her face. Aiming for an inhabited island, she travels as fast as her engine will carry her.

There, she can dock and find shelter. Call someone to let them know what is happening before her pursuers catch up with her.

But her boat is slowing down. Suddenly, the motor goes silent. *Shit.* She was in such a hurry to leave the marina in Cook's Cove that she forgot to check her fuel supply.

Quickly, she hoists the mainsail; it flaps lifelessly in the air, so she drops it. The sound of an approaching motor is growing louder. She searches the horizon. Several boats are hovering near the island's shore, but there isn't enough wind to escape. Panicking, she glances around for her phone. She picks it up, but it slips from her hand, and flies over the side into the water. She has to decide—stay and face who is chasing her or jump.

Wearing nothing but her wetsuit, Colleen takes a deep breath and dives over the side into the water, leaving her face mask and the tank behind. There's no turning back now.

Colleen begins to swim. *Don't panic,* she tells herself. Each stroke propels her forward, her limbs slicing through the currents with precision. The shore seems unreachable, but she refuses to let doubt detour her.

As she swims, her muscles strain under her exhaustion. The adrenaline that propelled her into the water is now turning against her, causing her muscles to tighten with each stroke.

Just when she thinks her strength is about to give out, an orange float splashes in front of her. She grabs it, clinging on as it pulls her toward a boat. Almost to its side, she recognizes who is waiting for her on deck. She freezes with fear, letting go of the orange object, and dives beneath the surface.

Chapter Six

Alice

"Mrs. Monroe? An Erin Citation thirty-four-foot sailboat registered to Colleen Monroe was found by the Coast Guard drifting in the water off one of the San Juan Islands. It was out of gas and the sails were dropped. A scuba tank and a mask were found on deck. But no one was on board."

"Colleen?" Alice utters, dropping to her chair. "She's missing?"

"I wanted to assure you the Coast Guard is now searching the area looking for survivors," the police officer tells her.

"This can't be true." She feels nauseous.

"I'm sorry, Mrs. Monroe. We promise we'll do all we can to find your daughter," the officer reassures her.

"My Colleen... You have to find her!" Alice is shaking as she hangs up. She reaches for a cigarette and a match, but she's trembling so much she can't light the end. She covers her face with her hands. *My baby is…* She isn't ready for another loss so soon. *No. They didn't say Colleen drowned, only that she's missing.*

Raising her head, she takes a deep breath. Alice dials Jody's number, her fingers fumbling over the buttons.

"What do you want, Mother?" Jody asks.

Tears welled up in Alice's eyes as she struggles to find her voice. "Jody, it's Colleen…She's missing. The Coast Guard found her boat abandoned. They're searching for her."

Silence hangs in the air for a moment, only broken by Alice's raspy breathing.

"What? Colleen's missing? Are they sure? I mean… what happened?"

Alice fights to steady her voice. "I don't know. We have to do something. We have to find her."

"Where are you?"

"I'm at the beach house in Cook's Cove."

"I'll come right away. I'm sure she's safe somewhere."

Alice ends the call, tears streaming down her face. She reaches for a cigarette and match again. Taking a deep breath, she manages to steady her hand enough to light the match, the flame casting a flickering shadow on her face. Placing the cigarette in her mouth, she inhales deeply. Every second counts. She can't bear the thought of losing Colleen. Damn it.

HER ELDEST DAUGHTER arrives at their beach house in Cook's Cove two hours later with her husband, Brian,

Taken from the Sea

trailing behind. Jody reaches out to console her mother, but Alice doesn't want to be hugged and pushes her daughter's arms away. She prefers to be left to her misery, not coddled like a helpless old woman.

"I've hired an investigator," Jody's husband offers, shifting his weight to his other leg.

"Who?" Alice turns to him, scowling. What's wrong with this man? She doesn't want Colleen's disappearance splashed all over the nightly news or the subject of a book about the Monroes. She needs someone she can trust to handle things with discretion.

"He's one of the best in Seattle," Brian smiles.

"I don't care who you hired. Get rid of him. I want Ben Stone working on the case." Alice reaches for her pack of cigarettes, pulls one out, putting it in her mouth, exhaling smoke through her nostrils like an angry dragon. Her thin, smoke-stained fingers tap a rhythm against the armrest.

"Never heard of the guy," Brian says, glancing over at Jody, who raises and lowers her shoulders.

Alice takes a drag, inhaling the pacifying smoke into her lungs, pausing for a moment, then exhales with the cigarette still in her mouth. "He's a local. A Native American man. I've heard good things about him." Several years ago, Alice learned that Ben Stone was a well-respected investigator specializing in missing persons, but often used unconventional ways of solving his cases. Some even thought he was a shaman.

She is acting superstitious, but damn it, if Colleen returned to the sea willingly, he'd be the one to tell her. Anyone else would assume she's crazy for thinking such a thing.

"Mother, must you?" Jody fanned the air, trying to dissipate the smoke. "It smells like an ashtray in here."

"It's my house. If you don't like it, you can leave." Alice takes another puff. Her cigarettes calm her. She's smoked since she was a teenager and isn't giving them up for anyone.

Jody shoots Brian a look.

"I still think my man from Seattle would be better," Brian says, rubbing his chin and lifting one eyebrow skeptically.

"Thank you for your opinion, Brian. However, I'm hiring Ben."

"As you wish." He looks over at Jody, who rolls her eyes.

Chapter Seven

Ben

Ben knocks on the door. He knew of the Monroes; however, their paths never crossed before. Most of his clients aren't as wealthy as the Monroes. Instead, they're just regular folks, hoping he can put their minds at ease regarding their missing loved ones. But he isn't going to turn away the money Mrs. Monroe is offering to find her daughter. It makes up for those he helps who can't afford his regular fee.

"Thank you for coming," Mrs. Monroe says with a tight smile, opening the door wide for him to enter.

She is in her early seventies, thin, wearing slacks and a sweater with pearls around her neck. She smells of Chanel No. Five and stale tobacco.

"This is my daughter, Jody, and her husband, Brian Gilbert."

Ben removes his Stetson and holds it at his side. He

extends his other hand, shaking everyone else's. Right away, he notices Jody as she eases herself into a chair, crossing her arms over her chest like she wants no part of this discussion.

Her husband, Brian, holds the familiar smirk that often greets him when someone discovers he's a sixty-four-year-old Native man, not some young, eager punk.

"As I mentioned on the phone, my daughter, Colleen, is missing," Mrs. Monroe announces, showing him to a chair in the living room. "I'd like you to find her."

"The Coast Guard found her boat abandoned," Jody adds softly, placing her hands on her chair's arms. "But Mother believes that she's still alive."

"Hmmm. And you don't believe that I take it?"

Jody cast her eyes downward and sighs without answering.

"Do you know why she took the boat out?" Ben continues watching Jody but turns when Mrs. Monroe answers.

"Because she's an idiot." Alice drums her fingers on the arms of her chair.

"What my mother means is that Colleen has a mind of her own and sometimes does things without letting us know."

"Like taking her boat out by herself?"

"Yes," Jody replies.

Mrs. Monroe gives her daughter a disapproving look. "I never wanted her to have that damn boat. It was my husband's idea that she learned how to sail."

"She's an experienced sailor and teaches sailing on Lake Washington in Seattle," Jody pipes up. "She's obsessed with the water."

"Yes, but the water on Lake Washington and Puget Sound are quite different," Brian adds.

"She's also into scuba diving and teaches a beginners' class for that, too," Jody says, shifting in her chair.

Ben nods, jotting down a few notes. "And this gives you a reason to believe she may not have drowned?"

"Yes," Mrs. Monroe replies. "She is an excellent swimmer and can hold her breath longer than anyone else."

Ben leans forward, his eyes fixed on Mrs. Monroe. "Do you know why she was out on the boat?"

Mrs. Monroe's fingers continue their nervous drumming on the chair's armrest. "I don't know. Colleen is a free spirit, always seeking adventure. Sometimes, she craves solitude, away from the constraints of everyday life. But she wouldn't just disappear without a word. Something must have happened."

He glances at Jody. "Have there been any recent conflicts or tensions within the family?" he asks, hoping to uncover any underlying motives or strained relationships that might shed light on Colleen's disappearance.

Jody hesitates, exchanging a glance with her husband. "Colleen can be a challenge, and we didn't always see eye to eye."

"Could you elaborate?"

"She's just different. Weird."

"How so?"

"She's irresponsible."

He smiles to himself. "Tell me more about Colleen's acquaintances or if you know of anyone who might have a reason to harm her," Ben focuses his gaze on Jody.

Jody shifts uncomfortably in her chair. "I can't think of

anyone who would want to harm her. She keeps to herself mostly. She's odd and doesn't fit in."

"Odd?" Ben wonders what Jody means by that.

Ben's eyes flicker between Jody and Mrs. Monroe, searching for subtle cues. "Well, let's just say she has different interests than the rest of us," Alice replies.

He has a hunch there's something they aren't sharing.

"Did she try contacting either of you before she left or while she was out on the water?"

Ben catches a glance between Jody and Brian again.

"Well... I didn't think it was important, so I didn't mention it to the police," Jody reveals, "but I got a text right after Colleen called me at work. It's before she disappeared. She attached a photo. It was a picture of a round thing, maybe a token or a button. I didn't pay much attention to it. She sent it with a message about calling the police if her friend Eric Lau didn't show up to work. But I deleted it. I thought she was just overreacting."

Jody continues, "Besides, it turns out there's a reason Eric wasn't at work. He turned in his resignation. I didn't see it until after I spoke to her, so I couldn't pass on the information. The email message said he needed to return to China immediately. That his mother was ill, and he didn't know when he'd return. He needed to care for his family, so he thought it best just to resign."

"Eric?" Ben raises an eyebrow and then writes the name down.

"Eric Lau. Her boyfriend or something. I don't know; maybe they just slept together. Her personal life isn't my concern." Jody shrugs. "He worked at Monroe Shipping."

"I see. And do you remember what the object looked like?"

"It was round and dark. I think there was an S on it."

"What if someone kidnapped her?" Mrs. Monroe interrupts, bringing her hand to her mouth. "What should I do if they contact me?"

"You'll let the police know if you receive a ransom note," Ben tells her. "They'll handle it for you."

"I can pay what they ask. I don't want anyone to hurt her."

"You'll have to work with the police detective on the case. But if anyone contacts you wanting money, don't just hand it over. A release must be carefully executed by the authorities so that Colleen is returned unharmed."

"Yes, yes. Of course." Mrs. Monroe fiddles with her hands in her lap, with her eyes cast down, looking at them.

Ben gets up. "I'll be in touch if I have any further questions." He'll come back when Mrs. Monroe is alone; she may know more than she's sharing at the moment.

DRIVING along the winding coastal road, Ben listens to the crackling voice of his detective buddy, Jackson, as he answers. The sun is dipping below the horizon, casting a golden glow over the water.

"Hi, Ben here. I just wanted to tell you Mrs. Monroe hired me to find her missing daughter," Ben says. She's been in contact with the Bellingham Police Department already. This isn't a competition; he and Jackson have previously worked on missing person cases together, so this one isn't much different. He'll share any pertinent information whenever necessary to avoid stepping on anyone's toes.

Jackson lets out a chuckle on the other end. "Great, you can deal with the old bat. I've had a run-in with her before. She can be a pain in the ass, so be warned."

"I appreciate the heads up, Jackson. I'll let you know if I find anything relevant to your investigation," Ben replies.

He hears Jackson sigh. "I may be the only one who cares at the moment. Here at the department, everyone thinks the girl drowned. And considering there is no evidence to indicate otherwise, the chief wants me to shift my attention to other cases and put this one on the back burner for now. We have a lot going on at the moment and are understaffed. Besides, she most likely fell overboard, and her body is on the bottom of Puget Sound somewhere. So it looks like you're on your own on this one, buddy."

Ben's heart sinks at hearing the lack of support from the police department. "Thanks," he simply says, ending the call and driving the last stretch home.

Stepping out of the car, he notices the sweeping view from his waterfront house. The moon is now casting a silver glow over the calm waters, whispering secrets only the night shares.

Upon entering his house, Ben puts his keys on the table by the front door, glancing at the pictures on his wall, which serve as reminders of the people he's reunited, and the mysteries he's solved over the years.

Going downstairs and settling into his home office, he opens his laptop. He's ready to dive into Colleen's life, meticulously examining every thread leading to her disappearance. But he soon discovers Colleen isn't on social media, leaving him without much insight into her interests beyond sailing and scuba diving.

He pores over the notes of the conversation with Mrs.

Monroe's family, hoping for clues. Glancing at the photos he took, he gains a better sense of Colleen's boat. But the images offer no definitive evidence of foul play, only raising more questions about what transpired the day she vanished. The odd thing is the boat was found clean of fingerprints except for those along a railing, which strikes him as highly unusual. The prints turned out to be hers, though. He doubts she wiped down the boat before going overboard. Someone may have boarded that boat, but who and why is a mystery.

Leaning back in his chair, Ben rubs his eyes. The long day is catching up with him. His mind churns over the scant information he has so far. This case won't be easy, but that only strengthens his resolve. Over his career, he's solved more complex disappearances with less to go on at first. Still, this one already feels different somehow, in an eerie, haunting way.

Shaking off the uneasy feeling, he goes up to the kitchen and makes some chamomile tea, hoping it will clear his head. As the kettle whistles, his thoughts return to the sea at night. So calm yet unpredictable. Just when you think you understand it, a rogue wave appears, stealing something precious, only to disappear into the dark depths once more.

What happened out there? Someone must know something that could crack this case wide open.

Chapter Eight

Alice

"Mother, Brian, and I are going to take off now. Give me a call if you need anything. I'll be in the office tomorrow," Jody says, giving her a quick hug before leaving with her husband.

Alice closes the front door behind them with a soft click that echoes through the empty house. A frown tugs at the corners of her mouth as the silence engulfs her.

She sighs and walks to the back deck facing the water, hoping the view will bring peace of mind. As she lights a cigarette with slightly trembling hands, visions of her missing daughter Colleen dance through her mind. She exhales smoke into the night air, eyes scanning the rippling waters, wondering if her baby is out there somewhere. Did Colleen fall overboard? Alice shakes her head slightly, not allowing those thoughts to fully form. She has to believe her daughter is alive and safe, that someone will bring her home soon.

Alice takes a seat next to the chair her husband died in. She coughs, spitting into a tissue. Looking down at the blood spot, she crumples the tissue and tosses it aside. The wind catches it, blowing the red stained tissue in the breeze, where it flutters above the water and sinks into the churning tide.

Sitting there, thoughts of the day she'd found Colleen drift into her mind. She'd been walking along the beach below this house when a noise in the wind grabbed her attention. A few steps later, she heard the sound again. Stopping, she turned around in a circle. In front of her was a large log washed up on the sand, so she climbed on top and gazed across the water. That's when she noticed a three-foot-long wooden box bobbing in the current about twenty feet out. When she heard the sound again.

She removed her jacket and sandals and waded into the water until she was close enough to touch the box. The noise—like a baying lamb—called out again.

Carefully, she guided the box across the surface until she could carry it in her arms. Once her feet touched dry land, she returned to the log and set the box down. Dripping wet, her clothes stuck to her, giving her a chill. However, she didn't care. Her curiosity was pushing her to peek into the box. The squeal was loud now. She crouched closer, with her hat shading the box from the sun.

At first, she assumed it contained an animal because of the fur lying across the top. Reaching in, hoping it wouldn't bite her if it were injured. But she found the fur to be loose, so she slowly pulled it back.

Her hand went to her mouth. It wasn't an animal but a tiny newborn baby.

"Oh, sweetheart, who left you here to be carried out to the cove?" She carefully picked up the infant. It was so small, with tiny pink legs and arms no larger than her fingers. A few threads of dark hair covered its bald head. Part of the umbilical cord was still attached.

The infant moved its head and made a face. Alice glanced around. No one else was on the beach. The baby couldn't be very old. It might even have been born prematurely. It appeared to be a girl. With no diaper or clothes, only a seal skin to keep it warm.

Alice slid her feet into her sandals and put on her jacket, tucking the baby inside, along with the fur. Clutching her precious bundle, she walked quickly to the steps leading up to her home.

Alice slid back the slider and went immediately to the kitchen. Taking a milk container from the refrigerator, she poured a small amount into a cup and warmed it in the microwave. She washed her hands, careful not to drop the baby, and sat cradling the infant in a chair. Then, she dipped the tip of her finger in the warm cup and put it in the baby's mouth. The baby began sucking. She repeated this several times, fearing it wasn't enough. She'd need to buy some formula soon.

As she watched the baby, her heart melted. Its little finger touched hers, and she knew she wanted the little creature more than anything in the world.

Going to the cupboard, she retrieved a basket and some towels and set the baby inside. Finding a flannel pillowcase in her linen closet to tuck around the baby. The infant appeared content, so she set the basket down and went to her wall-mounted phone. After picking up the receiver, she hesitated and hung it up again, unable to bring herself to notify the police.

Reaching for her pack of cigarettes, she walked over to the slider and stared blankly at the water as she smoked. After Jody turned six, she and Charles tried to have another child. But they waited too long. Now, she's in her forties and not able to carry a baby beyond the fifth month. And this little angel appeared. She couldn't just turn it over to some agency.

After pacing back and forth several times, Alice picked up the phone and called her attorney. "What do I need to do to adopt a baby I found?"

"You found? Mrs. Monroe, there are laws about taking other people's babies."

"I didn't steal it. The baby was abandoned on the beach. I think whoever gave birth to the child didn't want it."

"Well, you have a point. However, we still need to investigate who the mother is."

"I don't care. She's probably some irresponsible teenager who got pregnant, freaked out, and thought she could toss the baby like it's trash. I want you to find a way for me to keep it. I don't care what it'll cost. I want this baby!"

"Well, I'll see what I can do. I think, in the meantime, you should notify the authorities."

"I don't want them to take her away from me."

"Okay, okay… I'll talk to a few people I know in Bellingham and see what I can do."

As soon as he hung up, Alice dialed the number of Jody's pediatrician in Bellingham.

"I need to see Dr. Jennings and will be at your office in less than an hour. Could you please let him know in case he has to reschedule some of his appointments?"

"Is this an emergency? If it is, you should go to the hospital," the receptionist replied.

"Just tell him Mrs. Monroe will be coming in with a baby for him to examine."

Alice slammed down the receiver and turned to collect her keys from the kitchen counter. With the basket in her arms, she rushed to her car and settled the baby in the back seat, with the seat belt securely holding the basket.

As promised, she strode into the doctor's office within the hour.

"Dr. Jennings will see you, Mrs. Monroe. He's in room three."

Dr. Jennings looked up from the paperwork on his desk. "Hello, Mrs. Monroe. I've been told you have a baby you want me to examine. Is that correct?"

"Yes, she's a newborn." Alice set down the basket and lifted the bundle, showing him the baby's face.

He gave her a quizzical look. "I'm hesitant to ask, but what are you doing with this infant?"

"I found her abandoned in the water."

He took the bundle from her, set the infant on the table, and unwrapped the pillowcase from around her. "Abandoned. What a shame." He took the baby's temperature, listened to her heartbeat, then poked around her stomach.

Alice kept watching as he examined the infant. The poor thing is so tiny. She prayed that nothing was wrong with it.

Dr. Jennings smiled. "The baby appears healthy. She's

quite young. I would say this newborn is only a few hours old. It's a good thing you found her when you did. Being out on the water without proper care, she probably wouldn't live long." He cleaned up the umbilical cord and removed it.

Alice realized she'd been holding her breath. After deep exhaling, she said, "I'm hoping to keep her."

"Well, I'm sure you'd be a wonderful mother to this little creature. Not many children have the advantages you could provide," he said, peering at her over the top of the glasses resting on his nose.

"Thank you for your support, Dr. Jennings." Alice smiled, reaching for the child.

The doctor hung on to the baby. "Yes." He cleared his throat. "There is one thing you need to know about this little girl, though." He gently placed his hand on the baby's abdomen, and they both noticed something resembling a smile from the little thing.

"What?" Alice's stomach fluttered.

"She has a minor birth defect. It's called syndactyly." He showed Alice the infant's feet. "It means she was born with webbed feet. All babies have webbed fingers and toes in the womb, but they change as they develop. One in twenty-five hundred to three thousand babies are born this way. It's nothing serious. In most cases, it's genetic, so someone in her family must have carried the gene. When she gets a little older, we can cut the webbing. Her toes aren't fused together. She merely has excess skin between them. If you would like to wait, it won't affect her ability to walk."

Alice sighed. *Webbed feet.* She could deal with that. At least it wasn't something more serious.

The next day, when her husband, Charles, arrived home from his business trip, Alice told him all about finding the baby abandoned on the beach.

"So, you want to keep her. I take it?" He pulled the pink blanket slightly down to see the baby's face. "She's so tiny. Poor child."

"Yes. You know how much I wanted another baby. She would be a wonderful addition to our family, don't you agree?"

He looked at her with the baby in her arms. "I know how hard it's been on you. Both of us, really—not being able to have another child of our own."

"Please."

He smiled. "If it will make you happy, dear, I think we should consider what it would take to adopt her."

"Oh, thank you, Charles." She kissed him on the cheek, cradling the baby between them.

Alice was relieved that after her husband's phone call, the Sheriff told the officers only to conduct a casual search for the baby's mother. Her husband had also stressed for the police to keep information about the baby quiet so that the news agencies wouldn't get wind of it.

Within a month, the baby was listed as abandoned, and with Monroes' reputation and money, rules were bent, red tape cut, and baby Jane Doe soon had a new name—Colleen Monroe.

Chapter Nine

Alice

Alice is surprised to find Ben at her doorstep the following day.

"Hello, Mrs. Monroe. I came by to talk if that's okay." Ben smiles. He removes his hat and slips off his leather coat. She points to a hook by the door, so he hangs them there.

Alice sighs at his appearance. He's wearing jeans and a denim shirt. There's a design of a blackbird embroidered on the left side of his vest. His long hair is in braids, and there's a beaded choker around his neck. He is the best private detective in the area, she reminds herself.

He carries a worn leather knapsack with him and follows her to the kitchen table, where he retrieves a yellow pad and a pen from his knapsack and sits across from her.

Alice toys with a cigarette, changes her mind about lighting it, and leaves it on the table.

"So, what do you want to ask me, Mr. Stone?" She asks, curious about this man.

"Tell me why you believe Colleen is alive."

A flicker of emotion passes through Alice as she composes herself before speaking. "My daughter has a fascination with the ocean," she begins.

Ben looks up and nods, prompting her to go on.

"Colleen grew up around the water. We spend all our summers here. She'd never abandon her boat like that. She adored that thing. Half the time, she acted like a damn fish. Loved exploring the sea bottom and sailing. She was obsessed with it. So, it doesn't make sense that she'd vanish out there without a reason."

Ben stares at her with his deep brown eyes. "How was your relationship with Colleen before she disappeared?"

A pain of anguish ripples through her. Silence hangs in the air. She shrugs her shoulders and looks away as a tear forms in her eye. "I guess I did a crappy job of raising her. Too much money can make kids irresponsible. She turned out to be a free spirit." Alice let out a heavy sigh, then continued.

"It upset her when I told her she was wasting her life playing in the water. And it was time she acted like a responsible adult by honoring her father's wishes to go to work at Monroe Shipping." Alice looks down at her hands for a moment, then raises her head and stares blankly out into the room.

"It's what Charles wanted, you know. He thought it offered us security. It was his family's business, and he was proud of it. So, he was hoping we would too. I know we all have shares in the business, but now that he's gone, we are responsible for what happens there. I'm sure other people can make the big decisions. Still, we need to have a presence in the office," Alice explains.

She shoots Ben a sideways glance. "Jody thinks she can manage it, but I worry it's too much for her. And Colleen doesn't give a damn, but don't you go telling anyone that. We have a reputation to uphold, and I don't want people to think we're incompetent. If it's the last thing I do, I have to make this work. It's what Charles wanted."

Alice picks up the cigarette and lights it. She takes a deep inhale, then begins coughing uncontrollably. Jumping to her feet, she hurries to the kitchen sink and steadies herself, placing her hands on the counter. She runs the water, filling a glass. Once she regains her composure, instead of taking a drink, she drops the lit cigarette in the half-empty glass and turns to Ben.

"Are you alright?" He asks.

"Yes, it's nothing." She dismisses his concern and continues. "Colleen was supposed to meet me for lunch but never showed up. She didn't even text me to tell me she wasn't coming." Alice frowns. "I waited a half an hour for her."

"Perhaps she was gone by that time."

"Colleen could have told me she was going out on her damn boat," she grumbles. "Do you have children, Ben?" she asks, staring at him intently.

"A daughter," he replies.

"So, you know how wonderful they are when they're young. I'm afraid Colleen just doesn't want to grow up." It frustrates her that Colleen's always pulling away from her.

"Unfortunately, most children rebel against their

parents. They believe our ideas are too restricting and old-fashioned."

Alice humms. "I didn't want Colleen to throw away an opportunity many people would consider a dream job. I know it's nepotism, and she isn't entitled to a position. Still, how many women can step into leadership roles without clawing up the ladder? She could have the staff do all the work if she wanted. The business already runs itself. But Colleen didn't want that. No. She wants to play in the water instead. At least Jody appreciates what she has. Knowing the value of her inheritance." Alice shrugs. After a minute, she turns to Ben and asks, "Would you like to see Colleen's bedroom?"

The room is a mixture of childhood memories, teenage memorabilia, and stuff Colleen collected over the years. One shelf mounted on the wall contains books about coastal marine life. Ben browses them as Alice talks.

"Colleen has a degree in marine biology. However, she's never done anything with it. I wanted her to study something useful, like business or accounting."

Lined up next to the others are books on sailing. "Colleen dreamed of sailing in the World Cup, too. She entered and won several races out on the Sound. Even crewed on larger boats when asked." Alice grimaces when she read one title in particular: *Twenty Thousand Leagues Under the Sea*.

Stuffed animals—or rather, stuffed seals—sit on the bed. Alice remembers her five-year-old daughter making noises as if talking to the animals. In Colleen's make-believe world, they understood her. Claiming they were her family.

Alice picks one up, angrily tossing it across the room. She shouldn't have raised Colleen this close to the water, but Charles insisted they enjoy the same things he had during his childhood at this house. It once was a happy place to escape from the city, but not anymore. Now, it's nothing but an empty shell, a reminder of the past, of everything lost. She's alone in her pain. If only Charles was there to comfort her. To reassure her that everything would be okay.

She sinks onto the bed and begins to sob. The pressure of the world is getting to her. She needs to be strong, but inside she's afraid. Afraid she can't cope. With Colleen missing, she doesn't know how long she can keep fighting. Her fatigue is growing. This damn cold keeps lingering on and on.

Alice looks up at Ben, wiping her eyes. She's embarrassing herself in front of him. "I'm sorry." She stands up and blows her nose in a tissue. "I don't know why I did that."

"Don't be ashamed. Not knowing where your daughter is heartbreaking, I'm sure. Any concerned parent would be upset." He lifts the discarded stuffed seal, gently placing it on the bed.

"I've seen and heard all I need for now. I'll be in touch, Mrs. Monroe."

After Ben leaves, Alice pours herself a glass of wine, though it's early. But she doesn't care. Taking her wine, she steps outside and sits down. Her eyes go to Charles' empty chair.

This deck held many happy memories - barbeques with Charles churning homemade ice cream for dessert, his silly pirate songs and eye patch entertaining them.

Alice smiled slightly, remembering her daughter Colleen as a little girl, giggling as she flew up the steps, sand stuck to her from head to toe, hair a tangled mess. She would turn the hose on Colleen, having her lean over to work the twigs and debris from her dark hair. Then she'd brush the girl's hair gently, letting it dry in the sun to a shine like black silk. Unnaturally beautiful hair for a child, she thought.

Colleen was a wiggle worm, whirling around to music. Charles would sweep her up in his arms as they danced together. He spoiled his little girl, never suppressing her wild spirit. Instead, he just laughed and said she had a unique soul that needed room to be herself.

Alice finishes her wine in one long gulp, missing her husband. Missing their life together. Missing the family she once had.

Chapter Ten

Ben

Ben follows the stairs to the basement and turns on the light in his office. He picks up the framed photograph from his old oak desk; his wife, Paula, and their daughter, Sara, smile up at him. They are both dressed in the traditional garb of the celebration they were attending on the reservation. They are his skyhook that keeps him afloat during dark times. He misses them, but they are now in a place with no more suffering.

Their daughter died at the age of eighteen, strangled to death by the hands of a serial killer who kidnaped her. Ben vowed to find the man, but when he did, the killer had already taken his own life. Leaving revenge for the spirits that torment the soulless.

He let out a long, sorrowful breath. Six months later, a

stroke killed Paula. He sprinkled her ashes in the water off the coast of the reservation near Bellingham, so her spirit would mingle with the sea animals.

He married late but enjoyed having a family. It's coming up upon ten years now since he lost them. My, how the time flies, but the space in his heart holding the image of them remains the same. That's the funny thing about love; the memory of it isn't easy to let go of.

Ben returns the picture to his desk and gathers the notes from his interviews. His work keeps his mind busy. The missing makes up most of his cases. There are always clues as to what happened to these lost souls. The result of what he finds isn't always good, though. Unfortunately, they are often victims of foul play.

He pinches the bridge of his nose. He needs to focus on the missing girl with webbed feet.

Reaching for his phone, Ben composes a text to Tom Stapleton, his friend in the Coast Guard.

This is Ben Stone. I'm looking into the Colleen Monroe case. Any chance you can tell me what you know?

A few moments later, Tom replies:

We've already taken statements from all the boat owners and turned that information over to the Bellingham Police. But I can tell you no one reported seeing anything unusual. If that girl, Colleen, was as skilled on the water as everyone claims, she should've let someone know she was in trouble. Then there's the issue with her cellphone. It wasn't with the rest of her possessions.

Not looking good.

She most likely fell overboard. We've followed the currents, but I wouldn't expect to find her alive after this long.

Taken from the Sea

She could have gone ashore.

If she had, we would've heard about it by now. And the same goes for if she crawled aboard someone else's boat after going overboard. You'd think they'd report a rescue.

Well, thanks for your help, Tom.

Ben set down his phone. It's beginning to sound like everyone's given up hope of finding this girl alive. If Colleen didn't fall overboard, he'll need to find a reason for her disappearance.

Ben takes out a fresh sheet of paper, lays it on his desk, and begins to fill in his schematic. In the center of the page, he draws a fish to represent Colleen. Next, lines out from her to tether the people closest to her: her mother, Alice; her sister, Jody; and Jody's husband, Brian.

Alice Monroe is getting older, and though she'll never admit it, she is showing signs of an underlying illness. The stress of her daughter's disappearance probably isn't helping, either.

Ben sits back, rubbing his chin, pondering things. Jody mentioned that Eric Lau hadn't shown up for work because he quit and needed to return to China. If that's true, why was his not showing up for work a cause for concern for Colleen?

When he spoke to Jody, he'd picked up vibes that she wasn't telling him the whole story. Was it just sibling rivalry, or did Jody stand to gain something from her sister's disappearance? Her parents' business, perhaps?

He ponders the dynamics of Monroe Shipping. When the majority owner of a business dies, a lot of jostling can go on for power.

Jody's husband, Brian, also works at Monroe Shipping. Ben taps his pen several times on Brian's name; perhaps the man is hoping Jody will inherit the business if Colleen isn't found. Is he planning on taking over?

Ben stretches. The pieces aren't falling into place. He needs more information before he can solve this mystery.

Chapter Eleven

Colleen

Several days earlier

Colleen screams a stream of bubbles as a rope net curls around her. She's hoisted up in the air, then dropped onto the surface of a deck like a seal. As the net spreads open, a hood slips over her head, and she can't see. Someone peels off her wetsuit and grabs her legs. She kicks and flings her arms while a rope wraps around her wrists and ankles.

The hood over her head is removed. Somehow, she's ended up inside a cage. A tarp is thrown over her enclosure, and everything goes dark again. She closes her eyes and screams until her throat aches. The cool air is soon replaced with her own warm breath.

After a while, the lack of fresh air and the stifling heat causes sweat to drip down her face and sting her eyes. The combination of darkness, the smell of fish, and the motion of waves makes her heave.

Laying on her side with her hands and feet tied, she

loses all track of time, left with no idea how long they've traveled or in which direction. She tries going to happy times in her imagination, but all she can think about is what a screw-up she is. If she'd shown more interest in her father's business, Jody would've listened to her fears about Eric, and she'd be safe now.

There is an abrupt jolt. The engine goes quiet, and she hears movement. They are at the dock—that much she could tell.

The tarp is pulled off, and a bright light blinds her.

Colleen trembles from fear and the cold. Her chest is covered with her own vomit, and she stinks from relieving herself while lying in the darkness.

"My, aren't you a sorry sight? I should leave you in your mess 'til morning, but I think I'll clean you off."

A stranger attaches a hook to the top of her cage and flips a switch on a motor. The cable tightens and yanks her up in the air, where she swings back and forth five feet above the ground.

Colleen watches a man through the metal bars as he drags over a hose and points it at her. He moves his hand, adjusting the nozzle. Water shoots out, blasting her skin. She lets out a hoarse scream when the lukewarm water turns cold. "Shut it off, you idiot! It's cold, damn it," she croaks.

He chuckles, turns off the water, and drops the hose onto the deck.

Water drips through the bottom of the cage. Goosebumps scatter across Colleen's body, and her hair's a tangled, wet mess. Her teeth chatter. She tries adjusting her position but, tied up in this cramped cage, can only pull her legs closer.

The stranger lowers the cage onto a cart with wheels then removes the hook. "I guess without your covering, you're more sensitive to the cold, aye?"

The cage bounces as he drags the cart across the wooden boards of the dock over the dirt to a ramp to the front of what looks like an old shed. He takes a key from under a rock, places it in the padlock, and opens the door. He pushes her cart through, flicking on the lights inside. From what she can tell, it's a storage room. Nets hang on the walls, and faded floats litter the floor.

As he moves about, she notices that though he exhibits muscular upper body strength, his one leg is stiff, like something's wrong with it. He walks to a pile in the back of the building, returning with an electric heater. Once plugged in, the coils turn orange, and heat radiates out, taking away her chill.

He approaches her, unlocks the cage, and reaches in with a blade. "Don't you go and bite me now."

Her stomach is in knots. Is he going to cut her? She stays still while he slices the ropes with his knife. Once her legs are free, she flexes her feet, stretching her toes.

He touches her ankle with his water-stained leather glove. She flinches.

"Oh, look at your beautiful, flipper feet," he says.

Most men are shocked at the sight of them, thinking she's a freak. She usually wears socks when she sleeps with anyone; they could accept those better than her webs. But she's not cutting her feet to please a man. She likes them. They are part of her unique self.

The stranger slips his hand out and shuts the wire door.

Colleen moves to a sitting position, tucking her bare legs underneath her. She groans as the metal of the cage floor digs into her flesh. She'll have sores resting against these metal bars before long.

The man hums, watching her, and after a moment, he leans on a gnarled wooden cane lying on the floor next to him, pulling himself up, and leaves.

Colleen tries several different positions while he's gone; nothing is comfortable. Soon, the fisherman returns holding two towels in his arms and a foul-smelling tin bucket, which he sets on the floor.

"Maybe if you put this underneath, ya, you'll be more comfortable. He opens her cage and pushes them in with the end of his staff, closing the door afterward.

Weak and shaking, she lifts her bottom and shoves the towels under her.

"This way, when you soil yourself, it will be easier to clean you up."

Is he planning on keeping me in this horrible cage?

"I suppose you're hungry." After opening the door again, the stranger reaches around to the bucket, bringing out several small dead fish, tossing them next to her.

Their silver bodies lay in a pile, still dark eyes staring at nothing. She wants to gag, pushing them toward the door with her finger.

"Well, aren't you the fussy one? What type of fish do you like?" He puts one hand on his hip and raises the other, scratching his beard.

She didn't want to answer him, but she's hungry. "Cleaned, cooked fish," she mumbles, cocking her head at him. Her hair hangs over her shoulders, covering her breasts.

He bursts out laughing and slaps his thigh. "So, you're a

lady now, are ya? Changing your ways as quick as I can count now that you're out of your skin."

Colleen glares at him, wondering what the heck he's talking about. She's tired and wants to go home. Mustering what little strength she has, she pushes her fingers through the wire openings and, with both hands, shakes the cage violently.

"Feisty little bugger, aren't ya? I'll get you something else to eat if it'll make you happy. Don't want you starving to death."

He reaches his finger through a hole and scratches her shoulder with the tip of his glove. "I'll bring you some kippers in a bit. I need to tidy up my boat first." He steps out the door.

She drops her head to her chest as tears flow down her cheeks. Tired and afraid, she's never felt so vulnerable in her life before. Why is she here? What does this stranger want with her? If he is connected to those men chasing her, why haven't they shown up by now? Nothing makes sense. She closes her eyes to escape what she's experiencing. If she can imagine she's on the water, time might pass quickly, and soon she'll be free. In her mind, she sails into the sunset, listening to the sounds of the water lapping against her boat.

She loses track of time but lifts her head to the sound of a door opening. The stranger is holding a blanket and shoves it into her enclosure. It smells musty and is scratchy, but she pulls it over her shoulders, trying to cover up some of her body. After she is situated, he opens the door again and sets a plate of kippers in front of her. She picks up one and takes a bite.

"That's salmon. I dried it myself."

She eagerly eats the other pieces. Her throat is parched. "Can I have something to drink?"

He fetches a bowl, fills it with tap water from a sink along the wall, puts it inside the cage, and crouches down, watching her. Grasping the bowl with both hands, she brings it to her mouth and swallows it all.

After she sets the bowl down, he shoves a finger in the cage again, reaching for her shoulder like she's a pet. She moves away from his touch and glares at him.

"I'll leave you now so you can get some sleep." He takes the bowl and plate from her, relocking the cage. Using his cane, he helps himself up, walks to the door, and shuts off the lights.

Laying down in the darkness, she pulls the blanket around her neck. Exhaustion takes over, and she quickly falls asleep.

COLLEEN OPENS HER EYES, squinting against the harsh light that suddenly floods the small shed. She sits up and bangs her head, snagging her hair on the cage wires. Every muscle aches from being curled up on the cold, hard floor of the small wire cage all night. Her joints crack as she unfolds her limbs and attempts to stretch them out. But this confined space makes it impossible to fully extend her arms or legs.

She blinks several times before the blurry figure moving about comes into focus. It's the bearded fisherman from the seal island who pulled her from the water.

She glances around. Why is she in this contraption? Shit. This isn't a nightmare. It's real. She's in a damn cage.

Taken from the Sea

Colleen grasps the door and gives it an angry shake, the sound echoing around the shed. The man glances over at the noise but says nothing before lumbering outside.

She is alone again in this prison of rusted metal and damp wood. Colleen shifts, trying to find a position that doesn't dig the unforgiving wires into her already bruised flesh. But comfort is impossible to achieve. The edges of the cage poke into her side no matter which way she turns. She longs to stand fully upright. This cramped enclosure is suffocating.

Letting out a loud sigh, she rests her forehead against the cool metal in front of her. The events of the past day replay in her mind like a fuzzy dream. Was it just yesterday that she swam freely with the seals? It seems like a lifetime ago.

Now, her world is the size of this cage. She cranes her neck to glance around her dreary surroundings. The dingy windows let in only thin slivers of natural light. It appears to be a storage shed of some kind. Fishing nets, coiled ropes, and rusted tools line the walls. The permeating odor of fish overwhelms her senses.

This is no place to keep a human. She is not some wild animal to be caged up and put on display. The injustice of her imprisonment sits like a weight on her chest, making each breath a laborious effort.

As her initial shock and disbelief fade, a growing sense of dread fills Colleen. She has no idea where she is or why this stranger is holding her captive.

Tears sting Colleen's eyes as hopelessness threatens to consume her. She wipes at her cheeks. Crying isn't going to change anything right now. She needs to be alert and make sense of this dire situation. There has to be some way out of this nightmare.

A few minutes later, Colleen hears the padlock on the door click open. Her captor shuffles in, and he walks over. She recoils to the far back into her cage as she can. He still terrifies her.

"Let me out of here!" Colleen yells, hitting the side with her hand several times again.

"No, not yet." He laughs.

Yet? "So, when *will you* let me out of this thing?"

"When I feel like it." He crosses his arms in front of his chest, grinning.

She glares at her captor. He has a full beard almost to his waist and hair tucked in a navy stocking hat with a few stray strands poking out along the sides. His gray eyes are like the morning fog on the water. He's dressed in a worn brown flannel shirt, with a beige T-shirt peeking out from beneath. His jeans smell and are dirty, with the scales of dead fish sticking to the fabric above his knees where he rubs his hands. There are scuffed black rubber boots on his feet.

"My legs hurt. I'll be deformed if you don't let me out of here." Colleen tries to adjust her position as the metal bites into her, leaving a dark pink print on her skin.

"Oh, I hadn't thought about that. I don't have any bigger cages." The man looks around the room, eyeing the space. "Maybe I can build something."

Build something? And then it dawns on her: this man has no intention of letting her go. Instead, he plans to keep her captive like an animal.

She laces her fingers through the mesh, rattling it,

rocking back and forth. "LET ME GO!" she screams, all her fear and anger tumbling out.

He shakes his head. "No, I'm not doing that."

She swallows hard, shaking, breathing heavily.

Her emotions are all over the place. She wants this nightmare to end. What does he want with her?

Sobbing, she wipes her dripping nose with the back of her hand. "Do you want money? I can get you money," she offers meekly. He must know her mother would pay whatever he asks.

"I'm not falling for that. I'm not going to sell ya."

"I don't know why you're keeping me here, but I want to go home," she tells him between shallow breaths, pushing her hair out of her eyes. "Please," she begs.

He whacks the side of her cage with his thick, wooden cane. "Hey, you quit whining. I'll make you a larger place to stay, but I'm not turning you loose, so don't be asking me all the time."

Colleen shrinks away from the vibration of the metal and buries herself in the folds of the blanket. Moments later, the shed darkens, and she's alone once more. There appears to be only one way in and out of the building, and he locks that door. She closes her eyes and prays that she can find a way to escape this madman.

Chapter Twelve

Alice

Alice discards yet another bloody tissue on the table and lights a cigarette. As she inhales, her lungs barely fill before she blows out the blue smoke. She's tried drugstore cold medicines and cough suppressants, but they aren't helping her aching chest.

A prescription pill bottle sits on the table. It's for her nerves, but it only makes her dopey. It doesn't erase her fear. No one understands how she feels. How could they? She wants to know her baby is safe.

Ben told her he'd talk to boat owners in Bellingham to find out if they knew anything. She's pretty sure the police did that already, but Ben reassured her that more people trusted him than the police around this town, so if anyone had seen something, he'd be the first to know.

There's a rumor he's some sort of shaman. If she

Taken from the Sea

hadn't found Colleen on the beach, she'd assume Ben was just another person with their hand out wanting money. If he does have special powers, he may be the only one to tell her what she is afraid to hear.

Alice takes another drag on her cigarette. A coughing fit causes her to spew spit, blood, and smoke across the room. Her lungs ache constantly. She's having trouble climbing the stairs from the beach lately, running out of breath halfway. She should probably see a doctor, but they'll only lecture her again about smoking—like it's any of their damn business if she smokes or not.

Easing into a chair on the deck, Alice reflects for a moment. She should be grateful instead of angry. Her husband provided her with a wonderful life. This house was once a place of joy, but now it's just a reminder of the past.

She stares out at the water as it glitters in the sun, reminiscing about Charles.

They came from different backgrounds, but he never held it against her. Her parents were farmers in the Midwest, so the ocean was foreign to her, a mystery.

Her childhood was so different from that of her children. She wanted to give her girls everything she never had growing up. Her parents constantly worked to keep the farm running and didn't have time for her. Her father rose early and came back exhausted each night for dinner. Her mother worked in town as a bookkeeper and ran the house, cooking, cleaning, and doing the books. She remembered her mother always looking tired. That wasn't what she wanted for her future—to be a slave, just barely getting by at a meaningless job.

Her parents crimped and saved for her to go to college, and she set her sights far from home—on the West.

A week after graduating, she packed her bags and crawled into an old Ford pickup truck. Her parents were sad. However, they understood that their daughter didn't want the same life they had. They knew expecting a young girl to remain on the farm was a lot, so they gave her their blessings and waved goodbye. And so, Alice drove across the country, searching for a better life.

She remembered being amazed by all the trees in the Northwest and how green everything appeared. She never wanted to go back to Kansas. In Seattle, she would reinvent herself. Become someone with class and sophistication who wore nice things, not cheap discount items. She dreamed of living a wealthy life with servants and fancy cars. Believing it would bring her happiness.

Alice looks out at the water and takes a drag from her cigarette, remembering the expansiveness of her parents' wheat fields as both freeing and confining at the same time. The stalks waving in the wind were like the tide's ripples below this house.

As a child, she'd wondered what was beyond her golden horizon, longing to be near the blue of the ocean. But after traveling across the country to the Northwest coast, she found that the vastness of the water only represented unpredictability. Puget Sound, with its pockets and islands, provided something to look at, but beneath the surface was an undulating wildness that frightened her.

By chance, she'd met Charles at a party. He was much older, and his world was more expansive than she could imagine. He'd crossed the ocean and visited places she'd only seen on travel shows and in magazines. He was comfortable with different cultures and customs, introducing her to people she barely understood and cuisines she couldn't pronounce.

At first, she'd felt like she was in a movie, but her anxiety began to surface slowly. Playing the dutiful wife and attending dinner parties for important Asian clients soon lost its glitter. Traveling in a world she didn't understand, perfecting the mask she wore so no one would find out how fearful she was among them. Bowing and listening to their wives move around the room like skillful dancers while she stumbled over her two left feet. Inside, she was just a farm girl.

After years of pretending, she began distancing herself from her husband's friends, longing for a family to dote on. She was old-fashioned that way. After years of trying, finally, Jody was born. At last, she could play the role of mother.

Jody was well-behaved and content with studying and getting good grades. In the beginning, everything seemed fine. But soon, the urge hit her, and she became restless, longing for another child.

However, nature wouldn't cooperate, so years passed until she found Colleen, who turned out to be an entirely different creature. Funny that she would refer to Colleen as a creature. She had such dreams for that child from the sea —the girl with the webbed feet—born obsessed with the ocean.

When Colleen turned seven, Alice decided to take her to meet her parents in Kansas. Oh, did that turn out to be a disaster! Once they arrived, Colleen became unbearable. She thrashed about restlessly and wouldn't keep still, running around crying and yelling to be taken back home. She claimed she was suffocating and refused to eat her meals. Reasoning, bribing, and even threatening didn't work. She wouldn't get in after taking her to the local swimming pool to play with the other kids. Colleen whined that she wanted to go to the ocean and swim with the seals, not in a pool. Embarrassed by her child's behavior, the visit was cut short, and they returned to Seattle.

Colleen acted as if she was being tortured until they returned to Cook's Cove. And wouldn't you know it, the first thing the girl did was run down to the beach? Once she reached the water, she pulled off her clothes and waded into that disgusting tide. After that, she was fine. It's as though she were a different child.

As Colleen grew older, shaping her became impossible, with Charles filling her head with visions of adventure and travel. Alice shrugged her shoulders. They couldn't have been any more opposite in their ideas about how to raise Colleen. She'd wanted their adopted daughter to be a land lover like her, not a water sprite. Someday, Colleen would have to make tough choices to survive in this world.

Survive.

Alice put out her cigarette. What's wrong with her? How can she think those things when her baby could be lying at the bottom of the ocean at this moment?

Chapter Thirteen

Colleen

Colleen watches the fisherman haul stuff out of the shed—tools, wire, twine, netting, floats, and other things she has no idea what they are used for. Then, after a while, he pulls off his hat. His stringy locks, almost as long as his beard, make him look like a hairier version of the actor Jason Momoa.

She wonders how old he is—thirty, forty, maybe even older? He unbuttons his flannel shirt, throwing it to the side. His T-shirt is untucked, revealing tight abs when he reaches up. There is a mermaid tattoo on his left arm and a serpent on his right. The muscles in his arms flex as he lifts pieces of wood like they have no weight to them. After dragging a hand saw through the wood until each piece is the size he wants, he sets them aside. The guy works in his short-sleeve T-shirt until the underarms of his shirt are stained with sweat and the room stinks of perspiration and fish. But he always wears his gloves while working.

All day, the man works, fixing up this old shed while humming tunes she doesn't recognize. He gets around pretty well for someone with a bad leg. It's stiff; however, he's adapted to it. She wonders what left him with an injury like that.

Soon, boards are nailed together to make an eight-foot square box about three and a half feet high. Later, he drags in bales of hay, cutting the twine and spreading the straw around the base. She can't help but think his project looks like an animal pen. She expects him to bring in a few squealing piglets next to keep her company.

Colleen adjusts her position, trying to get comfortable. However, it's impossible in this small space.

Once the pen is finished, he carries in a worn, gray picnic table and two benches, dragging them across the room. He double checks the floor for any nails, picks up his tools, and sets everything outside.

Next, a large, galvanized tub that looks like it's for watering horses is set up along one wall. He drags a hose in, fills the tin from the sink, and shuts the water off.

Satisfied with his work, he opens her cage and motions for her to come out. "You ready to come out now and be a good girl?" the man asks in a patronizing tone. Colleen shudders. Out there, she will be at this stranger's mercy, vulnerable to unspeakable cruelty or worse.

"Come on."

She can't stay in this horrible cage. Colleen moves, dragging the blanket covering her along. Unfortunately, it won't fit through the opening, so she lets it go and crawls out naked on her hands and knees.

When she tries standing, her legs give out under her weight, and she lands back on the floor with a thump.

The stranger reaches out his arm for her to grab. She hesitates but then takes it. He swiftly pulls her onto her feet and swings her into his arms, causing her to shriek.

Undisturbed, he shuffles over and drops her into the tub. She doesn't know what is more shocking, his strength or the fact he put her in the lukewarm water. Goosebumps spring up along her body.

"Jeez, you could have made the water warmer."

"You've been living in the sea, and now you want warm water? Selkie, you're changing your ways minute by minute."

She splashes him. "I'm not a damn fish!"

He looks down at his wet T-shirt. "Oh, so you don't like being in this tub?"

"I prefer warm bathwater and want a towel to dry off when I get out." She's bluffing her confidence to find out what his reaction will be. Inside, she's scared to death of him.

He huffs, fetching a towel from a cupboard.

"I... I want soap and shampoo, too," she adds.

"You can wash with this." Pulling out a drawer by the sink, he takes a bar of soap and tosses it to her.

It feels like it will take her skin off if she uses it. Frowning, she slides down into the water, suddenly popping up again. There will be no lounging in here.

Throwing a leg over the edge, splashing water on the floor as she tries to get out of the tub. Seeing this, the man rushes over to the side and lifts her the rest of the way out. She hates being nude in front of this stranger.

His cold eyes scrutinize her shivering body, then he

grabs a towel and begins drying her off. Every fiber of her being wants him away from her, but her muscles seize.

Grinning as he runs the towel roughly over her naked body. Her throat tightens; she can't even muster the courage to ask him to be gentler.

Suddenly, he stops. From the corner of her eye, she sees him lick his lips. *Oh no. What's he going to do?* He drops the towel, reaching out a finger toward the nipple of her breast. She quickly brings her arms up, wrapping them around herself. "Don't you dare!"

His eyes lift and meet hers. Then he surprises her by laughing. Next, he scoops her up again, shifting his weight onto his good leg, and carries her over to the pen he created.

"This is your new home now. I'd get comfortable if I were you."

She is sitting on the straw, which jabs her bare skin, looking at the makeshift nest. "I can't sleep here." She frowns. In his mind, she is probably no better than a goat.

He let out a sigh. "It'll work for now, so quit your complaining." He throws a blanket at her and shuffles off, slamming the door behind him with a bang.

Colleen climbs out of the pen, pulling at the straw sticking to her skin. She picks up the blanket from the floor, wrapping it across her like a tube and tucking the end at her chest. Walking over to the only window that isn't boarded up, she looks out. The sun is starting to set on the water. She has no idea where she is in relation to her home. Are people looking for her? Sniffing her runny nose, she wipes her eyes with the back of her hand.

Wandering around the room, she finds a corner with a filthy shower curtain hanging to the floor. Pulling it back, she discovers a toilet, and immediately hitches up the blanket, and uses the facility. At least she has that modern convenience.

Colleen goes to the bench by the table. It's the only place to sit in the room. Resting her elbows on the wood and her chin in her hands, she raises her eyes. In the dim light, she takes in the grotesque shack that serves as her prison. The wooden walls are weathered and covered in grime. Dusty cobwebs stretch across the rafters. The floor is a minefield of dried fish scales and dirt. The place reeks of decaying sea life and oil. Cringing, thinking about the rodents that share this hellhole with her.

The only furniture is this stained, splintered table and benches he drug in. Near the table is a utility sink with a long crack running down the side. This is her world now and her life.

There's a noise at the door. She jumps up and backs away. The man shuffles in, holding a large, square container by its handles. He latches the door behind him then sets the container on the table. Unzipping it, he pulls out two bowls and a steaming pot of clam chowder. She's hungry, so she sits back down as far from him as the table will allow. He dips one bowl in and sets it in front of her, the other next to him. He takes the only spoon he brought and uses it himself, leaving her to suck her chowder out of the bowl.

Drops of chowder gather in the corners of his mouth and in the hair of his beard. He smells of fish. It's his perfume. That sweet smell that you either liked or it made you gag. It comes from his constant handling, cleaning, and eating fish.

Colleen isn't repulsed by his odor, though. Having

grown up around the smell of fish, it was familiar to her. Her father loved seafood and took her salmon fishing during the season. They also dug for clams on the beach together. When they returned home with a bucket full, her mother would put her to work cleaning the catch for dinner. She has fond memories of eating fish stew on the deck with her parents while her father told stories of their trip to Alaska - recalling the long days and nights spent wavering between harsh reality and fanciful dreams.

Sipping the creamy broth, she thinks about her mother. In her hurry to get away, she forgot all about their lunch date. Her mother is probably worried sick, wondering what happened to her.

Suddenly, all the events from the previous days rush into her mind—Eric's disappearance and being chased by those strange men. Is Eric okay? Is she still in danger? Locked up in here, she'll never know.

As the man eats, Colleen occasionally glances in his direction. She wonders about him. Why is he keeping her here? He appears lost in his thoughts. His hands, usually hidden in gloves, are scarred. When he notices her staring at them, he puts his free hand on his lap.

The man's hair is thick, and after a day's work, it hangs in unkempt strands. He looks like Santa Claus's evil twin. His eyes are the color of the sky, with a cloud passing over them. One minute, they give the impression the sun will soon appear; the next, a storm is brewing in the distance.

After they finish eating, he abruptly gets up and says, "I'll leave your breakfast on the counter tomorrow."

Tomorrow, Colleen repeats in her mind. *And the day after that, and the day after that.* She stares at the heavy, empty bowl in her hands, feeling its weight. Standing, grasping the rim, and placing her thumb inside, the wheels turn in her mind. His back is to her as he clears the other items on the table. She raises the bowl.

He whirls around. "I'd not be doing that if I were you."

Before she can slam it into his forehead, he yanks the bowl away from her.

Colleen realizes what a mistake it was when he grabs both of her wrists, holding them tightly. She flushes with fear. They both stare into the eyes of the other, waiting for one to flinch. His gaze bores into her so deeply he finds her vulnerability. His pupils dilate, and she experiences a strange pull, falling into his world. Finally, it is too much, and she looks away.

He lets go, gathers their dinner dishes, then leaves, turning the lights out behind him. The room is dark except for a glow from the far window that sends a beam of moonlight onto the floor, like a tether to the world beyond.

She moves toward it barefoot. The floor slants to the left, throwing off her balance and reminding her to use her sea legs to navigate the space. It's a man's storage room—just rough, uneven gray boards for walls, where cracks let the draft in. A few empty cupboards hang above the sink. There, she's expected to wash up; it's nothing more than a big utility tub with stains on the bottom. A wooden counter sits next to it, with cuts and holes. The room smells of everything stored there before--sweet and acidic, salty and smokey. And fish!

She walks over to the pile of hay, throwing a blanket across it to protect her skin, and then crawls on top with the extra blanket. God, what she'd give to sleep in a real bed with a comforter and sheets. To smell lavender instead of dust and mildew. To feel warm and safe. To hear her mother's voice again. She longs for the smell of cigarettes. And even misses her sister's snarky remarks and criticism. She thinks about her students showing up for the sailing and scuba lessons she isn't there to offer. And Eric, wondering if he is safe somewhere.

Staring up at the ceiling, she listens to the trees creaking outside and the clanging of wires from a boat—all the sounds of her new environment. Soon, tapping on the metal roof tells her it's raining. It comes in bursts like a ghost knocking to come in.

Pulling her other wool blanket over her head, hoping the night rodents don't burrow into the straw while she sleeps, she closes her eyes.

AFTER A FITFUL NIGHT of fighting the straw to get comfortable, Colleen discovers a bowl of warm oatmeal sitting on the counter that looks like glue. Still no spoon. Curling her fingers, she tastes the gruel. *Ick.* Not knowing when she'll eat again, she scoops up the porridge reluctantly, forcing it down.

Spending her morning looking for ways to escape, she comes up empty-handed. After searching the place several times, something she could use as a weapon or tool is nowhere to be found. Pushing at the nailed, boarded-up windows, trying to loosen the wood, she breaks the tips of her fingernails. The wood siding is soft in the corner of the room where dampness seeps in from the rain, but it only turns to splinters as she pulls at it.

She climbs onto the table, surveying the room, jumping down at the sound of a commotion outside.

The fisherman unlocks the door, entering with a mattress slung over one shoulder, which he drops on the floor, locking the door behind him. Once the door's secure, he pulls the lumpy thing across the room, flopping it down on top of the hay, sending straw and dust flying into the air.

She sneezes and pinches her nose.

"Is that better?" He glances over at her, standing there like a proud papa with his arms on his hips. There are no sheets or pillows.

"I guess so…" She stands with the blanket wrapped around her, wondering if there are any bed bugs in the mattress.

"I've got stuff to do now, so you're on your own."

Chapter Fourteen

Alice

The days are incredibly long, and she's bored from doing nothing but waiting for news--binge-watching movies on Netflix and reading several books, trying to distract herself. Not wanting to return to Seattle in case Colleen shows up.

Alice can't relax. Her throat is raw from chain smoking, and her voice is hoarse from leaving countless voicemails for Colleen. An overflowing ashtray sits on the coffee table next to crumpled tissues and an empty wine bottle. She hasn't changed out of her pajamas in days, wearing the same ratty robe and slippers she aimlessly wanders the house in.

The phone rings. Alice lunges for it, nearly knocking over the lamp on the end table.

"Hi, Mom." It's her daughter Jody.

"Have you heard anything? Are the police still searching for Colleen in Seattle?" Alice is praying for news.

"They went through her apartment and asked everyone a lot of questions, but she hasn't turned up. They did find a thumb drive under a chair. I told them it wasn't important. She took it from our beach house, and I would return it to you."

"Oh…" Alice eases down in an overstuffed chair, one hand supporting her head. She needs to go through her husband's stuff in the office but is putting that off.

"I'm at the office. And—"

"Yes?" She tries to sound interested.

"—Mr. Lei overrode one of my suggestions."

"What do you want me to do about it?"

"He just smiled but wouldn't let me explain why I thought my idea was the best choice. I reminded him that we hold the controlling interest in the company and that he is obligated to hear me out."

"Try not to cause too much trouble, dear. The man isn't your enemy, you know."

"Yes, mother. But—"

She doesn't want to hear about Jody's squabbles at work. The girl is a professional and needs to act like one. "Be patient with him. He may not like having a woman in charge." Alice rubs her forehead. A headache is forming.

"Yes, but he needs to respect me."

"You have to earn it. You can't demand it, honey." Alice wants to lie down and rest. "I'm tired. I'll talk to you later."

Alice shuffles to the kitchen for a glass of water to wash down an aspirin. Beyond the window, drizzle falls, and dark, gray clouds hang above. After swallowing the pill, she pulls open the slider and steps out onto the deck, letting the humidity moisten her hair and skin. She just wants this whole damn business over with—for Colleen to come home.

Trudging inside, she collapses onto the couch. The walls close in on her, amplifying the unbearable silence. She remembers all the conversations with Colleen in this room. Now, it's only stale air and her own ragged breathing.

In her hands, she clutches the Bellingham Police Department business card Detective Jackson gave her. She's lost count of how many times she's called for updates. Endless dead ends. Useless conversation intended to placate her.

"We're doing everything we can. These things take time. We'll let you know if anything develops."

Alice yearns to speak to Colleen just one more time, to know she's okay. She wants to apologize for the last argument about coming out here to their house on the water. Those angry words now haunt her.

With trembling fingers, she dials for the hundredth time to hear Colleen's outgoing message. "Hey, this is Colleen! Leave me a message!" Beep.

"Honey, it's Mom," Alice whispers. "I want you to know that you can stay at the beach house anytime you want. I just want you home safely. Call me please whenever you can. I love you."

She hangs up, knowing her message is likely in vain. But she doesn't want to stop trying. She'll leave as many messages as it takes for Colleen to know how desperately she needs to hear from her.

Alice glances up at the family photo on the wall, taken

at Colleen's college graduation. She looks so confident and full of promise in her cap and gown. Alice's heart swells with pride and longing.

Don't lose hope, she tells herself. The police will find her. She's a survivor, my strong, brave girl. Stay positive.

Chapter Fifteen

Colleen

Colleen awakens to the rattling of the door. She sits up.

A light sways, splashing shadows around the room, then stops when the lamp is set on the counter. The door slams shut with a thud, and she hears it being locked from the inside. The floor creaks.

Her heart is pumping wildly. *What is he doing here this time of night?*

The fisherman's body is staggering in the dim light as he makes his way to the bench next to the table.

"You awake, Selkie?" he asks, looking over at her. "I went to a bar in town tonight. You would've liked it. It wasn't like some of the seedy places I would go to in Alaska, where you could buy a woman for the night. No, these folks seem to care for each other. I watched couples dancing. Young gals with long hair—not as pretty as you—cuddling their bodies against their boyfriends, slowly dancing, and stealing kisses. After a while, it made me sad I couldn't be out there joining them. They seemed like they were having a great time."

Colleen adjusts herself, listening to him.

"I drank my whiskey and started feeling sorry for myself. It's been a long time since I've been with a woman, Selkie. I started thinking about you in here all by yourself. Your beautiful body, soft skin, long hair, and perky little breasts." He hummed twice in appreciation. "And how nice it would feel cuddling you. To taste you, touch you in that special spot, and make you moan. And ah-ha—to come inside ya. So, I decided to quit thinking about it and come here and make it happen." He began pulling off his shirt and boots.

Her heart is beating rapidly as her fear mounts. *Oh my God. This beast is planning on having sex with me!* Trembling, she turns away, pulling the blanket around her neck for protection.

He drags himself over, dropping his pants as he approaches. He yanks the blanket from her, exposing her nakedness. Afraid, she clutches her knees to her chest, hiding her face behind a curtain of hair, knowing it will provide no protection from him. The mattress shifts as he creeps closer to her. Nausea rises in her throat.

"Please, go away."

"Come here," his words slur.

In the pale light, she sees his bare muscular shoulders. He approaches her like some sort of wooly beast, smelling of booze and sweat. He pushes away her hair, and her body tenses when his beard touches her shoulder and his wet mouth grazes her neck. He runs his rough hands over her skin, sending shivers through her. She is petrified and angry at the same time.

When he turns her chin to kiss her lips, she hurls spit in his face. "Don't touch me. You disgusting creep!" she commands. *Oh God, what did she just say?* She holds her breath, expecting him to hit her.

He sits back, wiping his face with his arm. His eyes are on her in the darkness. He growls, "Jeez, what's wrong? Am I too ugly for ya?" He gets up, throwing the blanket at her. Limping, he picks up his clothes. Grabbing the lantern, he leaves, slamming the door behind him, locking it.

Colleen slumps against the boards, every inch of her body trembling uncontrollably. Snot and tears run down her face. She wants to cry out, but fear chokes her voice away. Pulling her legs in close, making herself as small as possible. If she could disappear entirely within herself, she would. Anything to escape this horrible reality.

She sits trembling, looking up at the ceiling, frightened of what the future holds.

She closes her eyes, praying again this is just a nightmare she will wake up from. But it's all too real. She is trapped here, at the mercy of a crazy man.

As she drifts into a fitful sleep, a single thought pierces the fog in her mind. If she doesn't find a way out soon, she might not make it out of here.

◻︎

COLLEEN EYES the fisherman warily as he limps into the shed, his shoulders slumped in apparent regret. She grips her blanket tighter at the memory of his unwanted advances the night before.

Taken from the Sea

Now he sits across from her, his bloodshot eyes peering at her from under his blue stocking cap. He slides a bowl of lumpy oatmeal in front of her, then reaches out as if to pat her hand reassuringly before thinking better of it.

Colleen stares down at her own hands clasped together on the table, struggling to contain the trembling anger rising within her. She will not give him the satisfaction of seeing her fear.

The fisherman sighs and looks away. "I thought you'd be happy to have me in your bed, but I guess not. I'm still figuring you out." He pauses. "Besides, I don't want you to hate me when I—"

He trails off, but Colleen knows what he means. He doesn't want her to despise him for whatever vile acts he is planning to commit against her will. The very thought makes bile rise in her throat.

"Hey." He wants her attention. "You're afraid of me, aren't ya?"

She reluctantly meets his gaze, her eyes flashing with defiance.

"I'm sorry about last night," he mumbles, glancing away as if ashamed. "I drank too much. A man gets urges…you know? But I ain't going to force myself on ya."

Colleen's jaw tightens. His pathetic excuses only amplified her disgust.

He looks over. His head is cocked to the side. "It's your body. Seeing you naked all the time makes me think about things."

Colleen gives him an icy stare and says, "For God's sake, then give me something to wear. I'm cold and uncomfortable like this." She gestures to the blanket wrapped around her torso.

"Sounds fair."

After a moment, he clears his throat. "I, uh, I'd best get to repairing those nets," he mutters, not quite meeting her eyes. He starts to turn away, pausing with one hand on the door. "I meant what I said. You don't need to fear me anymore."

The door clicks shut behind him, leaving Colleen alone with her turbulent thoughts. She stares at the closed door for a long time, hardly daring to believe what just happened. The memory of his assault is still fresh in her mind, but his apology caught her off guard. Perhaps he regrets his actions.

It's noon when he returns with a large bag in his hand. He throws it at her, and she catches it. Reaching into the paper sack, she pulls out two frumpy vintage dresses. One's faded blue, and another's green decorated with tiny flowers. Underneath are several packages of cotton underwear in size small that her grandmother in Kansas wouldn't even wear. Searching around, she didn't find a bra, though. Colleen looks up to find him pulling from his pockets a hairbrush, and a new toothbrush, and a tube of toothpaste, which he sets on the counter. Next, a box of soap and a bottle of baby shampoo.

He's watching her reaction. Colleen is confused. These simple items will make a big difference while being trapped here. She wants to trust him, to grasp any chance of getting out of here alive. But she can't afford to let a moment of kindness from him cloud her judgment.

"Now you'll feel more like a woman, I suppose."

Under her breath, she mutters a soft "Thank you."

He thumps the table, apparently pleased with himself, then leaves.

She gets busy trying on the dresses, settling on the blue one. They are too big, reminding her of the frocks she'd seen older women wearing in photos from fifty years ago. It would be nice to have a bra, but she's grateful for what she has. Dancing around the room, sighing with relief at not having to hide behind that scratchy blanket anymore.

Chapter Sixteen

Ben

Ben circles the name and taps his pen. What does anyone know about this guy, Eric Lau? What reason did Colleen have to worry about him? Who were his friends?

Mr. Eric Lau's been working for Monroe Shipping for a little over a year. The man studied business at the University of Washington, but after graduating with an MBA, he went back to China. So, why did he return to Seattle years later to work for Monroe Shipping?

Despite hitting dead ends while searching, Ben refuses to give up. He focuses on locating Eric's college classmates. After tracking down several, they mention barely knowing him, and they have no idea what happened to Eric after leaving the University. However, when he is about to give up, one man tells Ben he has something interesting to share but prefers to talk in person. So, Ben drives to Seattle to find out what the man has to say.

Ben parks his car in front of the old craftsman's house on Beacon Hill. The house is yellow with white trim. Two ceramic dragon heads with their mouths open sit on the side of brick posts at the top of the stairs leading to the front door. It's the part of town where many Asian people own houses. It has been gentrified over the years but retains its cultural flavor with an assortment of restaurants and businesses nearby.

Ben knocks on the door. A man answers.

"Sam? I spoke to you on the phone. I'm Ben Stone." Ben removes his hat.

"Yes, Ben. Please come in." The man opens the door wider for Ben to enter. Sam is a slim man in his thirties, wearing a Hawaiian shirt and tan slacks. His short black hair is tipped with red.

Glancing around, Ben notes Sam's place is decorated in bright colors—a red lacquered coffee table and an imported black Chinese chest embellished with traditional designs. Sky blue pillows big enough to sit on were piled in the corner.

"Please, have a seat." Sam extends his hand.

"Thank you for inviting me." Ben walks over to a yellow chair opposite a bright purple couch. He sits down, leaning forward with his elbows on his knees. "You mentioned on the phone that you might have some information regarding Eric."

"Yes, that's right." Sam nods, sliding onto the purple couch across from Ben. He clasps his hands together, seeming nervous. "But first, I wanted to ask - what do you know so far about Eric's disappearance?"

Ben rubs his chin thoughtfully. "Not much, unfortunately. I've been told that Eric requested personal time off to visit his sick mother in China."

Sam chews his lip. "I see. Well, that's interesting. I doubt he went back to China."

"So, where do you think he went?"

He leans forward. "As you know, I met Eric during college. We both attended the University of Washington together. But I'm more familiar with his boyfriend, Lee Jun."

"Boyfriend? I thought Eric was dating Colleen."

"No, Eric is gay. Well, maybe bi. I don't know. But Lee Jun has been his boyfriend for the last year until they broke up a month ago."

Ben raises his eyebrows, scribbling notes. This puts a new spin on things. "Go on."

"Well, before they split, Lee Jun told me he saw Eric talking with a man at Foo's Midnight Ladies Bar he suspected was connected to the Triad - the Chinese mafia. Lee Jun confronted Eric, but Eric told him to keep quiet. Said it wasn't safe to talk about it. People were watching. When Lee Jun called to apologize, Eric never returned his calls. So, Lee Jun went to Eric's apartment to find out why he was getting the brush off and found a woman there."

"Colleen?" Ben asks.

Sam shrugs. "He didn't say. But he saw a Triad coin on Eric's table. It's a dragon inside a circle."

"Interesting." Ben is processing what Sam is telling him.

"I haven't heard from Lee Jun since he told me about the coin. I'm afraid something happened to him. Something awful."

Ben leans forward in his chair. "What makes you think that?"

"I went to check on him after he didn't return my call. He has a cat, and when I got to his place, I heard the cat meowing, so I used my spare key and went in. The litter box was full—like a week's worth of shit. It looked like the cat hadn't been fed in a while and had broken into its food in the cupboard; dried food pellets were scattered all over the floor."

Sam rubs the top of his hand with his thumb nervously, then continues. "I poked around. His clothes were still in the closet. When I checked the refrigerator, I found containers of moldy takeout food. Lee Jun would never have kept that in there. He was meticulous. And later, I learned Lee Jun hadn't shown up for work either. He works at Foo's, and no one's seen him or heard anything from him."

Ben could hear the desperation in Sam's voice. Ben hums. "That doesn't sound good...." He furrows his brows as he takes more notes. "And now both Eric and Lee Jun have disappeared?"

"Yes. I'm worried." Sam twists his hands together. "I'm afraid Eric got mixed up in something dangerous."

Ben taps his pen on his notepad, deep in thought. "Have you told the police your suspicions?"

"No." Sam shakes his head. "I have no proof. And to be honest, I'm afraid of what might happen if I say too much. The Triad don't mess around."

"I understand," Ben replies. "Thank you for telling me this. It's extremely helpful for my investigation. For now, let's keep this between us until I learn more. I don't want you taking any risks."

Ben gets up, tucking his notes into his jacket pocket. "You've been a big help."

They shake hands, and Ben lets himself out.

───

IT'S dark by the time Ben pulls up outside the neon-lit exterior of Foo's Midnight Ladies. He slides a small high-power flashlight into his jacket pocket. Time to start asking questions.

The interior of the bar is a mixture of glitz and the absurd. Andy Warhol-type posters of women painted in glow-in-the-dark colors hang from the walls. A handful of men sit drinking at tables. The pink-haired bartender in drag is drying glasses with a rag at the bar.

Ben gulps: he is definitely out of his element in here. He takes a seat, laying a 20-dollar bill on the counter. "Gin and tonic, please."

The bartender glances at the bill. "Haven't seen you here before." He slides Ben the drink. "I'm looking for someone who comes here often. Young Chinese guy, name's Eric." Ben watches the man's reaction closely. "Know him?"

The bartender shrugs. "Lots of guys come and go."

Ben sips his drink casually. "Well, if you remember anything, give me a call." He slides his card onto the counter.

A voice bellows behind him. "Why are you asking questions about Eric?"

Ben turns to see two heavyset Chinese men looming over him with their arms crossed.

Ben stands slowly. "Just a concerned friend looking into his disappearance. Know anything about that?"

The men laugh, glancing at each other. "You don't strike us as Eric's type."

"We don't like nosy friends," The other one growls.

This isn't good. Ben is a sixty-plus, straight Native American man in a gay bar next to two unhappy thugs. Time to make his exit. He gets up and edges towards the door.

But the men block his path. "We're not finished talking to you."

Ben's mind races, assessing the situation. The two thugs are clearly out to intimidate him.

"Look, I don't want any trouble," Ben says evenly. "Just let me walk out that door, and you won't see me again."

The men sneer. "Can't do that. I think the boss would like a word with you." One cracks his knuckles menacingly.

Ben's hand slides towards the flashlight in his pocket. "Yeah, well, you can tell your boss I'm not interested."

In a flash, Ben whips out the flashlight and shines the blinding beam directly in their faces, incapacitating them. They become disoriented as they raise their hands, shielding their eyes.

Ben barrels past them, shoving through the door and bursting into the night air. He sprints to his car like he is being pursued by the devil, keys ready.

Chapter Seventeen

Colleen

When the fisherman walks in the door and announces, "I brought you something." She comes over to see what he has.

There's a flat box tucked under his arm. He sets it down and opens the lid, dumping hundreds of pieces onto the table.

Colleen gives him a quizzical look. Is this some sort of peace offering?

"In case you've never seen one, this is a puzzle." He points to the box lid. "It will look like this when it's put together."

Colleen takes the lid and inspects it. There is a picture of an old-world map on it.

"I thought this might be something for ya to do." He

gives her a sheepish smile, then says, "I can help start it." He smooths out the pile and picks up a couple of pieces.

Well, this is totally unexpected. Grateful that he's trying to make up for his previous behavior she relaxes her shoulders and decides to just go with it.

Colleen hasn't put a puzzle together since she was a little girl. He studies each shape and begins snapping them together.

"I take it you've put this together before," she says, studying the pile.

"Yes, many times." He looks over at her with gentle eyes. "I've got others when you finish with this one."

Colleen watches him as he assembles one side.

He stops. "It's your turn now."

She moves her hands through the pile, searching for a piece she thinks might work. He walks over and stands behind her, looking over her shoulder.

"That one." He points to an odd shape. Colleen feels his breath on her neck, making her shiver. She picks up the piece and places it where it belongs. Then she eyes the pieces for another. Her stomach flutters with him standing so close. Part of her wants to run and get as far away from him as possible. But strangely, another part wants to stay.

Colleen picks out a piece, turning it as she examines the border, moving it this way and that, trying it out. He places his hand on her shoulder. Her body tightens, but his face holds a smile, and his eyes twinkle. Sensing he isn't going to harm her, she relaxes.

"I've got stuff to do." he squeezes her shoulder.

After he leaves, Colleen starts working on the puzzle. Although in her mind, she has another puzzle, she is trying to find the correct pieces too. Just when she thought she had this stranger figured out, he no longer fits in that space. She hasn't seen any evidence that he works for the men after Eric. If this man isn't a monster, a rapist, or a psycho, what is he?

After bringing her the puzzle, Colleen finds a small spark of hope growing inside her. With time and patience, maybe she can convince him to let her go. It is a slim chance, but it is all she has to hold on to.

Going to the window, she peeks out. It is her only glimpse of the world beyond this room. Rubbing her bare arms up and down nervously. It has been too long. If she could just dip her foot in the water, feel the coolness, walk out, and let the tide hug her body. She has to find a way—soon.

WHEN THE FISHERMAN brings dinner that night, he looks like he's taken a shower and washed his hair because it is still damp. He made salmon steaks, boiled potatoes, and a salad for them to eat and even brought silverware--no knife though, but a paper napkin for Colleen.

After setting two mugs on the table, he opens a thermos, pouring what smells like hot cider into the mugs. He throws his leg over the bench and sits down.

"That cider's got rum in it, so there's a kick to it. I thought it might help you relax."

"Oh." Colleen isn't going to drink any, afraid he might be planning on getting her drunk.

He gulps his mug, then sets his arms on the table and stares off into space while he eats like Colleen isn't in the room.

Tired of just having conversations in her mind, Colleen asks, "Do you have a name?"

He glances over at her. "MacGregor."

"Is that your first name?"

"No, it's Jason. But everyone calls me MacGregor." Jason takes a long drink from his mug, then wipes his mouth with his sleeve.

"What happened to you?" Colleen points to his leg.

"Why do you want to know?" Jason's eyebrow lifts, and he adjusts his body, so he is now angled toward her.

"Just curious." She takes a bite of salad.

"I was working on a commercial fishing boat in Alaska." Jason slips a fork full of salmon in his mouth, washes it down with a drink from his mug, and says, "Got me leg caught in the ropes."

As Jason tells his story, Colleen catches herself feeling sorry for him. His life sounds sad. She can tell the alcohol is affecting him and isn't sure how Jason will act after the last time she saw him drunk. However, tonight, he seems to be friendlier and less threatening. Still, she has her guard up.

"Do you own all the property around here?" She is curious about how far her prison extends.

"No, not all of it."

"Have you lived here a long time?" Colleen tosses her hair over her shoulder, rests her chin on her hand, and listens to his answer.

"A few years. This once belonged to Frank Hall, an old codger in his eighties. I met him at the bar while living in a shack after my accident. Hall and I would get drunk and talk about how the world was going to hell, and we wanted no part of it. I guess he purchased this place back when no one cared about living out here. He didn't want his land cut up and have a bunch of snobs living on it. So, he drew up his will and put my name on it as the person to inherit the property. And when Hall finally died, I became its owner."

Colleen nods politely. "Were you ever married?"

Jason takes a long swallow from his mug, then wipes his mouth with the back of his hand. He stares off into the room. "Yeah. Once, when I lived in Alaska, but she ran off with someone else." He gives out a humph. "What woman wants to be with an ugly man with a gimp leg who smells like fish all the time?" Jason asks, taking another drink from his mug.

Something stirs inside her—pity, or is it compassion? Jason has a hole in his heart, thinking he is unlovable. Colleen wants to reassure him he isn't that bad and not to give up hope. She doesn't, though. Feeling sorry for Jason isn't going to fix her situation any. He is her captor, after all.

"Where are we? Are we on the mainland or an island?" Colleen asks.

Jason's demeanor changes. "You ask too many questions." Without another word, he gets up and packs up their plates and mugs.

"When will you let me go outside?" She asks as Jason heads for the door.

"When I can trust that you won't try to run away." The door closes, and Jason locks it from the outside.

⊏⊐

THE NEXT DAY, Jason arrives with a round piece of metal with a hinge in one hand and a canvas bag in the other.

Colleen gives him a wide-eyed stare.

"Sit down," he points to the bench. "Gimme your foot."

She can see what he plans on doing with it and crosses her arms in front of her chest. "No."

"If you want to go outside, I have to put this on you."

"Just let me out. I won't run away."

He laughs. "If you want to stay here, that's fine with me. I just thought you might want some fresh air."

Grinding her teeth, she sits on the bench with her back to the table and reluctantly gives him her right foot.

He clasps the cold metal around her ankle and locks it. Next, he opens the bag and takes out a chain that he runs through the ring at the side.

She sighs.

"Come with me," he motions for her to follow. They step out the door together, with him holding the chain off the ground.

The light is blinding, and Colleen quickly raises her hand to block the sun's rays from her eyes.

Breathing deeply, she inhales the fresh air greedily. The birds are singing. The sun is in the sky above. She looks down at her own shadow and lets out a long breath. Finally, she can see where she is.

Turning slowly in all directions are trees. A small wooden house sits nestled among them. It is a humble, one-story wooden structure like you might find next to a mountain stream. No decorative plants out front needing attention, only a small wooden porch and sandy dirt. But near the door is a single wild daisy. She goes over to it and squats; it is just a little thing, but it is growing here of all places.

Colleen stands up. To the left is a short path leading to the dock. A light post rises on one side next to a crane, and a fishing boat gently rocks on the other. All around, green trees reach up like giants, spreading their arms out and intermingling with the others. Closing her eyes, she takes a deep breath of the pine-scented air. Silently saying a prayer, thankful to be outside near the water. She can't survive without the water nearby.

She opens her eyes again when Jason speaks.

"I own most of this property around here," he points, moving in a circle. "I don't much care for neighbors, as you can tell."

There are no other dwellings, as far as she can see.

"This way," Jason points to a space between the trees, letting out a length of the chain so she can walk ahead of him.

An opening reveals a path that leads through the woods. The dirt is soft and damp from the shade beneath her feet. As they travel away from the house, a light flickers through the trees like a spirit glimpsing them as they walk. Birds flutter, and forest animals scurry away.

Gingerly walking down the path barefoot and dragging the chain behind her, Colleen finally can hear the water splashing against rocks, making her spirits soar. Water. As they round a corner, the bright sun pokes out from behind a white cloud. She stops, bringing her hand up, shielding the sun, as she surveys the area.

Large boulders go from the shore into the ocean, and smaller, flatter ones lay scattered on the sand. To the left, years of erosion have washed away the side of a higher bank, creating a cliff of dirt that has become a home for birds to nest. The spot is secluded, and the rocks hide the view boaters might have if they paid attention to the shoreline as they traveled by. Nevertheless, it is a beautiful spot, and she'd be delighted to explore the area under different circumstances. However, she won't go far with a chain attached to her leg.

Jason points to a flat rock, lifting the chain for her to go in that direction. Once they reach the rock he is interested in, he moves his hands around it, searching for something. When he finds the metal ring embedded in the rock, Jason pushes the chain through the opening and brings it back around. Next, he takes a padlock from his pocket and fastens it.

So, this is going to be her prison yard. She walks around, testing how far she can go before she reaches the end of her chain. It isn't far, but the good news is that she is outside instead of stuck in that dreadful shed and can touch the water.

"I'll be back later," Jason calls as he walks up the trail, disappearing back into the woods.

She inhales the aroma of kelp and iodine, sea urchins, and decay. The scent tingles Colleen's nostrils, filling her with possibility. It melts her stress like sea glass smoothed by the ebb and flow of tides.

The thin blue-and-white cotton dress she wears flaps gently against her body in the breeze. Strands of her long hair tickle her face. She tastes salt on her lips. In the distance, boats travel the waterway. Lifting her hand to shade the sun, she watches vacationers, fishermen, pleasure boats, and an occasional ship carrying containers go by. Waving would be useless; she is too far away.

She submerges her feet in the cool wetness. Ahh. She lets out a breath. God, she has missed the feel of the tide on her toes. The buzz of a seaplane overhead draws her attention, and she looks up. Immediately, she searches for rocks. Finding only small ones the size of her palm, she quickly lays them out in the sand, spelling S.O.S.

Standing back, she bites her lip. There is no way her distress message can be read from above. Discouraged, she kicks sand at her pathetic call for help, then picks up several rocks, throwing them in the water. She goes over to a flat area and sits down. *I'm never going to get out of here!*

Colleen stretches her body out and stares at the sky, watching clouds form into different shapes. One takes on the appearance of an angel before it slides apart into wisps.

A grunting sound on the beach brings her attention back to the water. Three seals are coming ashore. She sits up as they wiggle their bodies closer. Are those the same ones who crawled aboard her boat? Yes, she recognizes one. So how did they know where to find her?

The largest of the three waves its neck back and forth and barks. The others crawl onto the nearby flat rocks, get comfortable, and look out at the water like the regal ladies they are, watching over their kingdom.

Colleen pulls up her knees, wrapping her arms around herself. She tries imitating her companions, but her bark sounds more like a dog's than a seal's, making her laugh. While watching the seals, her worries crumble, leaving with the outgoing tide. A meditative state embraces her, like a hug from another world. Don't be afraid is the message the seals are telling her. We are here with you.

She listens to the tide slap against the rocks and watches the water glistening in the sunlight. Two gulls dance in the air, gliding on the wind. One climbs higher, and the other joins it. Together, they head out to sea like a couple on an adventure.

Colleen feels a presence nearby and turns to find Jason

sneaking up quietly behind the rock she is on. There is a bucket in his hand. She starts to get up, but he motions for her to stay and not say anything. She wrinkles her brow. What is he up to?

When he reaches her, he hands her the bucket. Inside are several small fish.

"It's for your lady friends," he whispers, pointing to the seals.

"Oh." She smiles, picking up a fish by its tail. She barks to get their attention, quickly tossing a fish. One seal catches it and moves closer, signaling the other two seals to the meal Colleen holds for them.

Glancing over at Jason, she can tell by the grin almost hidden behind the hair on his face this pleases him.

After several minutes, Colleen hops down from the rock and hands the empty pail back. The ladies push their bodies back into the water and disappear into the tide.

Jason unlocks her chain from the rock, and they walk back to the shed. Colleen won't be able to explain what happened, so she says nothing. She is sure whatever he thinks took place only confirms his idea that she is something other than what she really is.

Chapter Eighteen

Ben

After poking around the marina in Cook's Cove, Ben thinks about what Sam told him. Jody mentioned a photo of a coin bearing an S. It probably wasn't an S but a dragon—the symbol used by the Triad—the same coin Lee Jun mentioned seeing at Eric's place.

Unanswered questions are whirling around in his mind. Did something happen to Eric, like Colleen mentioned? Maybe he crossed the Triad somehow and is now dead? Was Colleen's life in danger when she disappeared? Why did she take the boat out in the first place? Did Colleen plan on meeting Eric out on the water somewhere?

While driving back to Bellingham, Ben takes the freeway off-ramp and is sitting at a stop light when his phone rings. He puts it on speaker.

"Can you hear that?"

He frowns. "I'm sorry, who—?"

"This is Alice Monroe. Listen."

Ben doesn't hear anything other than the surrounding traffic. "What is it I'm listening for?"

"There's a boat cruising close to the coastline. This is the third time they've passed by. I've been watching them through my binoculars. Hold on. I can see them now; two are in the boat."

The light changes and Ben slows down as he approaches the next intersection. "Can you describe them for me?"

"They look to be on the heavy side. One's wearing glasses. Oh no."

He grips the steering wheel tighter, though he fights to keep his voice calm. "What?"

"One of them is pointing to my house. If I felt better, I'd go out there and—"

"No," Ben interjects quickly. "No, I don't think that's a good idea. They aren't coming ashore, are they? I'll come right over if you don't feel safe," Ben offers.

Alice clears her throat. "I don't know what they would expect to find here if they came ashore. I wish they would go away. Should I call the police?"

He knew they wouldn't come unless she was being threatened. "I don't think so. There is nothing they can do about it anyway. Chances are the boat will have disappeared by the time they arrive. Can you call and ask someone to stay with you for a few days? I don't like the idea of you being there alone." These might be the same thugs he's crossed paths with while in Seattle.

"I guess I could ask Jody to stay with me."

"Call her."

"Have you found anything about Colleen yet?"

He doesn't want to tell her he is the only one trying to find her daughter right now. "When I do, I'll let you know."

BEN GRABS a beer from the refrigerator and goes to his office, his mind racing. Taking a long draw from his beer bottle, he thinks back to the mysterious men Alice saw at her home. The idea that a boat was out on the water outside of Alice's place concerns him. Were they Triad goons looking for Colleen? If so, there's a good chance she didn't drown, but she is hiding close by instead. What could they possibly want with a young girl like her? Money? No one's come forward with a ransom demand yet, which he finds odd. Maybe they have a different goal—something to do with Monroe Shipping, perhaps.

Sitting at his desk, Ben takes out a pen and a legal pad, drawing a circle in the middle of the page. Instead of putting Colleen's name in the center as he usually would, this time, he writes "Monroe Shipping." He draws lines radiating out from the circle, labeling the spokes: Charles Monroe, Alice Monroe, Jody Gilbert, her husband Brian, and Mr. Lei, the partner, and Eric the friend.

He scratches out the principal owners, Charles and then Alice. Tapping his pen several times. That leaves Jody, Brian, Mr. Lei, and Eric. He starts to cross out Eric's name but then hesitates. Was he eliminated because he knew something, or is he in hiding, too?

The coin comes to mind. Was it a warning? If the Triad wants to muscle in and take over the shipping business, they'll need to eliminate a few key players—like the Monroes.

This brings up the question of Mr. Lei. He could either be a mastermind or a pawn. In either case, Lei stands to benefit from the removal of the Monroe women.

Alice would be no problem. Her health is declining, and she is backing away from the responsibility. Colleen holds shares but isn't active in the business. If Colleen is eliminated, her shares will roll over to Jody. Ben underlines Jody's name. Jody's either part of the scheme or will soon be another victim of it.

There are many pieces to this puzzle he needs to find before he has a clear idea of who is behind this.

Placating Mrs. Monroe is becoming a challenge. She hired him to find her daughter, so he needs to focus on that part of the equation at the moment.

Ben rubs the bridge of his nose before picking up the phone to call Detective Jackson. "Could you have someone keep an eye on the Monroe residence?" he asks.

"Why?" Jackson questions.

"Alice Monroe called saying she spotted some men spying on her house from the water. They may have been looking for Colleen. I don't have proof, but I suspect Colleen's disappearance might be related to Mr. Monroe's death and Monroe Shipping. If I'm right, Mrs. Monroe and Jody could be in danger." Ben's hoping Jackson will put in an appearance so Alice Monroe has some assurance that the Bellingham Police Department is working on Colleen's case.

"Anything's possible. But I have my doubts. The chief wants me to focus on other cases. He doesn't like chasing dead ends because Alice Monroe wants us to. She's been a real pest, calling all the time. Besides, everything points to her daughter drowning. He believes these are two different cases—the daughter's disappearance and what happened to the father."

"I understand," Ben replies, though his gut is telling him they're tied together.

"I'll drop by and check on Mrs. Monroe, but that's the best I can do for now. You'll have to provide solid evidence to support your theory before I can do anything else."

"Sure." Ben sighs. "Any news about Mr. Monroe's death?"

Jackson lowers his voice. "You never heard this from me but Seattle PD took over Charles' case since he was a prominent businessman there. But I learned someone from his office picked up his prescriptions in Seattle. None were the poison that killed him, according to his doctor. So, they suspect the pills were switched or tampered with at the pharmacy. The pharmacist was at lunch, and his replacement took a bathroom break when it could have happened. None of the people they talked to saw anything. The person picking up the prescription was shopping in another part of the store and swore they didn't touch the bottles because they were in the bag. The tainted bottle got tossed, so they couldn't get any prints. As you know, without any evidence, it's hard to prove who did it or whether it was an accident or deliberate."

Ben gazes out his office window, processing the information. "Too many questions unanswered if you ask me," he mutters.

"Well, keep me posted if you uncover anything about the girl," Jackson says before hanging up. Ben puts the phone down, feeling frustrated by the lack of answers in both cases.

BEN STROLLS to the back of his house, looking at the water. It is time to take out his canoe to look for clues hidden from everyone's eyes. The truth beneath the lies— the ones we tell others and ourselves to explain what we don't understand.

Pushing the canoe into the incoming tide, he jumps in. Picking up his paddles and reaching through the current, stroke after stroke, he recreates the path of his ancestors as they left to harvest fish from the sea. Looking up at the sky, he thinks of Colleen. He has to see her as his daughter, not some rich lady's child, and use all his gifts to find her. He silently vows to take her from the wolf's den in combat if necessary.

He stops and takes a breath. A breeze tickles the surface of the water, sending ripples across it. There is an evil presence in the air—he can sense it. It moves like a hungry predator, curling around the trees, searching for the same thing he is—a lost child. A mother is weeping, like so many other mothers, wondering where their daughters have gone when they don't return home at night. The mother bear and the doe, the coyote and all the animals of the forest, the birds in the sky, and the fish in the water. We are all connected; we do not mourn the loss of our children alone.

Setting his paddles in the boat, he drifts in the current. Then, closing his lids and quieting the noise of his thoughts, Ben releases his crow spirit into the air. He searches in his mind's eye, looking for signs Colleen is alive.

His spirit soars up into the clouds, circles, and swoops back down, landing on the branch of an evergreen tree overlooking a secluded beach. Seals are sunning themselves on the rocks.

Taking flight once more, the crow spots a nearby house hidden by trees. A dock with a fishing boat tied up sits in the water. But there's no sign of people milling about nor a woman fitting Colleen's description. Still, there's something here—unclear emotions in muddled waters—but not death. Instead, life obscured by a lie.

The bird returns, and Ben lets the spirit back into his heart, and he paddles back home.

After dragging his canoe to the shore, Ben sits on a log outside by his firepit. He listens to the gentle rhythm of the dancers in his mind. He raises his hands and calls upon the wisdom of past chiefs.

Patience, preparation, intuition.

His ancestors pound the dirt and whirl in their costumes. They chant of the hunt. Ben joins them in spirit, then lets out a whoop. The space between the past and the present, the real and imagined, fades into the shadows.

Chapter Nineteen

Colleen

When Jason walks in, Colleen gets up from the table and asks, "Do you have some magazines or books? I'm bored and need something to read." She has no idea if Jason reads and, if he does, what his collection of reading material consists of.

"You can read?" His eyes widen at her request.

She hisses, "Pff. Of course, I can read."

He hums, scratching the side of his face. "I might be able to come up with something. I only have old books, though. Nothing you might find interesting."

"How do you know? I might like them."

"I'll bring you a box, and you can go through them and pick out what you want."

Later, Jason enters, holding a cardboard box filled with books, and sets it on the table. She claps her hands, beaming with excitement. He stands back while she pulls out several. Jason is right; the books are old—worn, too, like they've been read many times.

"Thank you." She gives him a quick glance and a smile.

He winks. "I'll leave you to choose what you want to read."

Rummaging through the box, she discovers they are about life on the water—her favorite topic. Pulling them out one at a time, she stops when she finds a small book titled Myths of the Sea and sets it to the side. There are so many to choose from that she can't decide which one to read first.

After an early dinner with Jason, Colleen washes her other dress in the sink, sloshing it around in the bubbly warm water and wringing it until all the soap is gone. Next, she sets it on a rack Jason gave her.

Her hands are red from being in the water. She stares down at them, remembering how she once had weekly manicures, doing her nails in different colors, like yellow and purple. The black she last painted them wore off. The bottoms of her feet have toughened up without shoes, and her toes spread out more, revealing the webbing between them.

Reaching back, she grabs her hair and braids it, slipping an old rubber band she'd found on the floor over the end. There's no mirror to see what she looks like. Not that it matters. No one would recognize her without her dark eye makeup or trendy clothes, especially her mother. At this moment, she probably looks like a peasant from another time. Yet, strangely, she is more comfortable like this, less pretentious.

Settling on her mattress, Colleen opens *Myths of the Sea*.

Inside, the paper is wavy from being exposed to moisture. A few pages are smudged and stained a light brown color. Skimming through sections, she finds it filled with ancient tales about old sea legends. Going back and slowly turning each page, she stops where the binding's cracked, revealing the hand stitching holding the paper together. The word 'Selkie' in swirling calligraphy is at the top of the page on the right. Below is an etching of a mermaid sitting on a rock.

Curious, Colleen reads the story. It's about a fisherman who finds a selkie—a seal that steps out of its skin, revealing a beautiful woman inside. The fisherman takes her home and hides her skin so she can't return to the sea. He makes her his wife, and their children are born with fin-like feet.

Colleen brings her hand to her mouth and looks down at the skin between her toes. *Oh, my God, I bet Jason believes I'm this mythical creature.*

She closes the book and glances around the shed where he is keeping her. What kind of man believes such nonsense? He isn't stupid, but can he be trusted if he believes she's an animal?

Colleen crawls under her blanket, but sleep evades her. She is restless. The walls are closing in on her. Her skin is dry, and she craves saltwater. After adjusting her position several times, she gives up.

It's dark in the room except for the glow from the small window. Dressed in the T-shirt Jason gave her to sleep in, she crosses over to the light and peers out into the water lit by the moon. The stars cast a ribbon of glittering tears across its surface. She lets out a loud sigh. In the distance, she hears barking, then the sound of a boat engine. Is that Jason?

Sweat breaks out across her skin. She is suffocating. She needs to touch the water. She taps on the window then pounds it with her palm. "Let me out of here!" she yells as the pressure builds inside her. Her skin, her mind, her whole being is desperate for saltwater.

Whirling around, she goes to the cupboard and opens the door, looking for something to break the pane. She has to get out of here! But the cupboard is empty of anything large or heavy enough. *Damn.*

Returning to the window, she brings up her arm, hitting it repeatedly against the glass. Her knuckles are aching and bruised. A crack finally appears in the glass. She slams her fist against it again, and a V-shaped piece breaks off and falls to the floor.

Reaching her fingers through the hole, grabbing one of the remaining pieces, glass slices through her palm. Pulling on the broken piece again, it cuts deeper into her. She screams out of frustration and pain.

A moment later, there is a commotion at the door, and it flies open, banging against the wall. Jason holds a flashlight, bouncing a tunnel of white around the room. The beam lights up her face, then her body. She is clutching her bleeding hand.

"Jesus, Selkie, what have you done?"

He switches on the overhead light and pulls her over to the sink; she doesn't resist. The fight is gone from her. He turns on the faucet and runs water over her bloody hand.

"Hold the cut together." He pinches it, showing her what he wants her to do. "I'll be right back." He rushes out the door, leaving it wide open.

Colleen stares for only a moment before running to the door then out into the darkness. With gravel beneath her bare feet, she takes off through the gap in the trees down the driveway. She starts sprinting.

The pain in her hand is throbbing, and blood flows uncontrollably. *Shit.* She can't leave like this, a bloody mess in a T-shirt. If she manages to escape and someone finds her, they'll think Jason tried to kill her, and she doesn't want them to think that. She freezes when a light shines at her from behind.

"Selkie, what the hell are you doing?" He approaches her, and just like that, she begins to cry.

"Come here. We need to take care of your wound."

Sniffing back her tears, she reluctantly walks back to the shed with him.

Jason holds a first-aid kit. He takes out some antiseptic and sets it on the table. "Come sit down and give me your hand."

By now, the front of her nightshirt is soaked red with blood. She obeys. He opens the bottle of antiseptic, and she squeals in pain as he pours it into her wound. Then he blots her hand with a clean cloth.

She jerks her arm back at the sight of the needle and thread he's holding. "You're not going to sew my hand, are you?"

"I'm not taking you to the doctor. You can bite on this if you feel the need." He hands her a piece of gauze. "Give me your hand."

She puts the gauze in her mouth with her free hand and gives him her other, turning away, squeezing her eyes shut.

He pushes the sterilized needle into her skin, pulling the thread through repeatedly as tears drip down her face. Then he wraps gauze around her hand and tapes it closed.

Jason packs up his kit and then tells her, "You would've

never gotten out that window. It's too small. And you could have bled to death trying to find your way out of here."

Her lips tremble. She looks up at him. His eyes are sad. A pang of guilt hits her in the gut. She let him down.

"Take that thing off. I need to wash it before the blood sets." He points to her shirt. "I'll get you a clean shirt." He leaves, soon returning with a fresh T-shirt in his hand.

Tugging at her bloody shirt, she finds her bandaged hand isn't any help. "Can you please help me, Jason?" She drops her head and stares at the floor.

He slowly slides the shirt up, running his warm hands along her torso, the sides of her breasts, and her upstretched arms, pulling it over her head. She shivers at his touch, biting hard on her lip. He tosses the bloody thing aside.

Now naked and vulnerable, Jason looks down at her feet, slowly raising his head, taking in every inch of her body. He reaches out and touches her seal tattoo next to her stomach with his forefinger, and she quivers. His eyes linger on her breasts, noticing her nipples are tight, he smiles.

Jason turns away and picks up the clean shirt. He helps her guide her raised hands into the holes and brings the fabric down, pinching it between his thumbs and forefingers. He spreads his other fingers, purposefully dragging them across her bare skin down the sides of her breasts again. Her body lights up. She lets out a gasp. Goosebumps scatter across her arms. Facing each other, his gray eyes look deep into hers. She knows he wants her.

Fighting her growing urge, she begins to sweat. In her mind, she's begging him to touch her again, desperately wanting to feel his hands on her, caressing her. She gulps. *Can he sense what she's feeling?*

He moves his lips, "Ahh, Selkie. If only…" he whispers.

She tilts her head, reaching out her hand to touch his beard.

Jason backs away from her, shakes his head, and leaves, locking the door behind him.

Colleen drops her arm, takes several deep breaths, then cries as confusion sweeps over her.

Chapter Twenty

Alice

Alice leans in as Jody kisses her on the cheek.

"Are you all right, Mom?"

"Thank you for coming this evening. Ben thought I should have someone here after seeing a couple of gawkers in a boat go by. I didn't like them out there spying on me."

Jody lugs her suitcase through the door with her laptop bag. It appears to Alice that Jody will be setting up a makeshift office here.

As Alice is about to close the front door, Brian sticks his arm out, stopping her. He walks in carrying a suitcase.

"Oh, I wasn't expecting you." Alice backs up. She'd been hoping it would just be her and Jody.

"We drove up separately. I'm only staying the night, then heading back to Seattle. We can't leave running the company to Mr. Lei, can we?" Brian says, winking at her.

Taken from the Sea

Alice isn't that fond of Jody's husband. He's a bit controlling. However, it's nice that he cares about Monroe Shipping. God knows her mind is on other things now, and she needs someone else to take that responsibility off her shoulders.

Brian follows Jody to her room to get settled. Alice walks past, pausing in the hall, when she hears voices drifting through the open bedroom door.

"I'm worried about Mother. Now she's imagining that people are spying on her."

Brian scoffs. "If she'd followed my advice and hired a professional investigator, we'd have this wrapped up by now."

After listening in on their conversation, Alice returns to the kitchen to pour herself an early glass of wine. Perhaps she is fooling herself by believing Colleen is still alive. If her daughter is dead and not merely missing, she needs closure. She's not giving up hope until Ben thoroughly investigates every possibility.

"May we?" Jody takes the wine bottle sitting on the counter and pours two glasses, handing one to Brian.

"I've dropped off some flyers in Cook's Cove for businesses to put in their windows," Brian says, swirling wine in his glass. "I thought offering a hefty reward would flush out someone with information. I listed the number for the Bellingham Police Department as a contact. They can screen the calls."

Damn him. Why did he go and do a stupid thing like that? "Swell, once a reporter finds out my daughter is missing, it'll be all over the news." She takes a drink. "You had no right to go and do that without consulting me first. That's why I hired Ben. I want to keep this quiet."

"Mom, he's only trying to help," Jody pleads.

Alice glares at her daughter. "I just hope this doesn't reflect badly on our business."

"I'll send out a notice telling all the employees to refrain from talking to the press," Jody assures her.

Alice lets out a loud sigh. The last thing she wants is people snooping into her family's life.

"I should also let you know I'll be out of the country for a while," Jody announces. "Mr. Lei would like me to fly to Hong Kong to meet with some clients."

Alice frowns. "What? They can't fly here?"

"No, he wants me to meet with them in person so they can show me around."

"He is the one who deals with China these days. He speaks the language. I don't see why he can't go."

"I thought Brian could join me. It would be a mini vacation for us. I've always wanted to see Hong Kong."

"When are you leaving?"

"Not until next month. That should be enough time to wrap up Colleen's case," Brian replies.

"Yes, we wouldn't leave until we know for sure," Jody adds.

"What? That she's dead?" Alice shuts her eyes.

"No, mother."

She feels Jody touch her arm and brushes it off. "It's what you think, isn't it? That I'm a fool for believing otherwise."

"It's just that…."

"I know. You don't have to tell me." Alice places her glass down and looks over at Brian. "As far as Hong Kong goes, you do what you think is best." She isn't up to arguing anymore, so she leaves for her room and closes the door.

Taken from the Sea

After falling asleep, Alice wakes to a sound coming from outside. She hears voices. Grabbing a flashlight from the drawer by her bed, she steps out into the darkness.

"Colleen?" she calls.

There is rustling in the bushes. She points the light in that direction, slowly taking a stair at a time until she is standing on the sandy dirt. She calls again, "Colleen, is that you?"

The porch light turns on, and Brian steps out in a robe. "Alice? What are you doing out here?"

Alice turns. "I heard something."

Brian comes over, takes the light from her, and flashes it around the yard, bouncing it off the foliage surrounding the house. Something moves in the bushes close to where the cars are parked. Brian carefully walks in that direction. The light he is holding lights up a pair of eyes, and a raccoon scurries off.

Alice lets out the breath she has been holding. It wasn't Colleen. She slumps her shoulders, looking off into the woods while Brian goes back inside. She hears him mumbling. "Your mother should see someone. This is ridiculous, going out and chasing down every noise at night."

"Shh, Mother might hear you."

Alice stands there a moment, then the unmistakable sound of branches breaking sends her heart rate soaring once again. Damn, Brian, for taking the flashlight with him.

"Hello?" she calls.

There is no reply.

There is the sound of footsteps on the gravel driveway. She rushes to the cars, but it is dark, and whoever it was disappeared into the night.

THE FOLLOWING DAY, Alice sits in the quiet stillness of her husband's study. She flips through an old album of their life, a feeble attempt to find solace in memories when the ringing of the phone shatters the silence.

Startled, she reaches for it. "Hello?"

"Mrs. Monroe? This is Dr. Harper from the county medical examiner's office."

"Yes, Dr. Harper," Alice replies. "Is this about Colleen?"

There is a brief pause. "No, Mrs. Monroe. It's about your husband. We've completed the toxicology report, and I'm afraid I have some unsettling news."

A cold dread seeps into her veins. She remembers a required autopsy report on her husband's death. "What is it?" she asks, her voice barely above a whisper.

"The tests revealed the presence of a poison in your husband's system. Digitalis, to be specific. It's a substance that can cause heart failure in high doses," Dr. Harper explains, his tone clinical yet empathetic.

The room spins around her, and Alice grips the edge of the desk for support. "Poison?" she echoes. "Are you saying my husband was murdered?"

"It's a strong possibility we cannot ignore," Dr. Harper continues. "Given these findings, we're moving this case to a homicide investigation. I'm truly sorry to deliver this news over the phone, but we felt it was urgent."

Murdered. The word echoes in Alice's mind. First, Colleen's disappearance, and now this. How much can she take? She buried her husband after what she believed to be a sudden heart attack. Now she is being told he was poisoned - murdered.

Who could have done this? Why would someone want Charles dead? Did Charles discover something troubling related to a client? Stumbled onto some damaging information? Try as she might, Alice can make no sense of why someone would poison her husband.

Dr. Harper's voice sounds distant as if coming from another world. "Mrs. Monroe, are you still there? Do you have someone with you right now?"

She hadn't spoken for several moments. Forcing herself to respond, "Yes, I'm here," she manages to say. "My daughter is here with her husband."

"I'm glad you're not alone right now," Dr. Harper replies kindly. "I know this is devastating news. Please make sure you have help around you as you process this. And we'll need to talk more about this soon, but for now, please take care of yourself."

After a few more exchanges, the call ends, leaving Alice in a stunned silence. She collapses into the desk chair, sobbing into her hands as the photo album slips off her lap, pictures of their smiling life together scattering across the floor.

She doesn't hear Jody enter the study but spots her standing in the doorway.

"Mom?" Jody rushes to her side. "What happened? Did they find Colleen?"

Alice can barely speak. "Your father…he was… poisoned…murdered."

Jody's eyes go wide. "Murdered? Daddy? Are you serious?"

She nods. "Dr. Harper just called."

"Oh my God."

Brian appears behind Jody, filling the study doorway. "What's going on?"

Jody turns to him with a helpless look.

Fresh sobs wrack Alice's body before she is able to recount the call she just received from the medical examiner's office.

Jody and Brian listen as she tells them Charles was poisoned with a substance that killed him by cardiac arrest.

Jody embraces her tightly while tears spill down her cheeks. Alice finally lifts her head from her daughter's shoulder with a shuddering sigh. She holds Jody's hands tightly in her own, grounding herself in the present moment.

"We need answers," Alice says, her voice edged now with an insistent demand. "We need to find out who did this. For your father's sake."

Jody nods. Brian steps forward and puts a supportive hand on Alice's shoulder. "The police will sort everything out, don't worry. We'll get justice for Charles," he assures her.

Brian is probably right. She just needs to understand why this happened and if Colleen's disappearance is somehow connected to her husband's death.

Chapter Twenty-One

Colleen

It's claustrophobic in the shed. Colleen is going stir-crazy. Jason isn't going to let her out until her hand is healed. His excuse is that he is concerned that if she sits out on the beach, she might get sand in her bandage, causing an infection.

She pulls Myths of the Sea from the box of books and takes it to the table to read. Halfway through a story about a Kraken, a giant octopus, Colleen hears the rumble of a motor outside. However, it doesn't sound like Jason's boat. Besides, he told her he wouldn't return until later in the afternoon.

Curious, she sets the book down and goes to the broken window. Jason nailed a scrap piece of wood across it, but there is a sliver between the boards, where she peeks out.

A stranger's boat pulls up to the dock. She listens. Two

men are talking while they walk. Their muffled voices grow louder as they get closer.

"What will you say if someone's home?" one man asks.

"That we're looking for a dog that ran off. No one would question that."

She hears their footsteps leave the boardwalk, then a rattle at the shed's door. She freezes.

"It's padlocked. I don't think anything's in there but junk, anyway. Let's go check out the house."

Curious, she stands by the door quietly. Now is her opportunity to get out of here. She could be free. Desperately wanting to say something, her throat tightens. Something isn't right about what they said.

Colleen listens, wondering who those men are. If they're the police, they would have driven down the driveway, not come by boat. And if those men know Jason is gone, why are they still here? After a while, she hears footsteps again.

"Well, she's not here. We better move on to the next place."

Colleen brings her bandaged hand to her mouth. Are they looking for her? Could they be the men who chased her in Seattle? If only she could get a better look at their faces.

She presses her ear to the door, straining to hear the men's retreating voices. One of them laughs. "The boss isn't going to be happy we came up empty. We better keep looking." Their footsteps retreat down the dock.

She listens anxiously until the boat's motor fades into silence. Peeking out the window again, she scans the water for any remaining sign of the intruders.

She paces the shed, gnawing a fingernail. Jason's books

sit abandoned as scenarios skip through her thoughts like stones across the water. Jason's absence has made her feel vulnerable. Being taken back to civilization might not lead to the freedom she is hoping for. Here, at least she has Jason reminding her of better days on the water.

That evening, when Jason brings their dinner in, she wants to tell him everything. She really does. But once she sees his piercing gray eyes, she can't. He probably wouldn't believe her anyway and think her story was made up, so he'd let her go. She'll have to keep everything to herself a while longer. Besides, Jason is lost in his fantasy about her and may not react kindly to the truth.

THE NEXT NIGHT, Jason checks her hand, cradling it in his lap taking the bandage off. It's healed enough to remove the stitches, so he carefully pulls them out. Though his hands are scarred, they are gentle, and there is a tenderness in his touch. A strange attraction is pulsing through her, and she wonders what his face looks like underneath all that hair.

Recently, she spied on him through the tiny space in the window after he'd returned from a catch. It was a hot day, and she watched as he pulled off his long johns; a nice muscular body was hidden beneath them. He sprayed down his torso and legs with the hose to cool off. The picture in her mind brings a mischievous smile across her face.

Jason looks over at her. His eyes sparkle. "Well, it doesn't look like you'll have a scar."

She lets out a sigh. If she is ever going to learn about Jason, she needs to get him to open up. "Jason, what was your childhood like?"

He cocks his head and gives her a curious look. "My childhood? You want to know about my childhood?"

"Yes." She smiles. "I want to know all about you."

"I doubt that." He shakes his head.

"No, really. Tell me about your childhood."

He scratches the side of his face. "Well, I was born in a small fishing town in Scotland. My mother died in childbirth, along with my baby sister. After that, I went to the docks with me da, where some wives of the other fishermen stepped forward to take care of me until I was old enough to go to school. Then Mrs. Mackey took me in while my father was out fishing. She made me do my lessons, so I learned to read and do math."

Her smile drops. A sudden sadness washes over her as she listens.

Jason stares off into the room while recalling his memory. "Wanting to be like my da, I'd sneak aboard the boat. When he caught me, he'd tell me I was too young, and that fishing was a hard and lonely life. He insisted I stay out of the way. But I still envied him. He was my hero. Often, I'd wait at the dock for his boat to return. When I was older, I'd ask the men to put me to work hauling in the catch. Slowly, they began to trust me and gave me more to do."

She is beginning to understand why he is so independent. It sounds as though he'd pretty much raised himself.

"But one day, when I met the boat, my father wasn't there. Another fisherman told me a wave had swept my da out to sea. That night, I walked back to our empty house, packed my bags with books, and stole away on a ship. I was fifteen but lied about my age. After that, I worked my way

Taken from the Sea

across the ocean. A mate I met suggested we go to Alaska to find our fortune." Jason scratches his beard. "You know the rest."

Having grown up with a mother and father who loved her, his life sounds empty.

"Did you ever miss not having a family?"

"Aye," he confesses, giving her a sideways glance. "I'd hear other men talk about their families back home and wish there was someone waiting for me." He watches her. "It's something I've always wanted."

Colleen bites her lip, then looks down. She feels sorry for him. Silence fills the room for a moment.

Jason lifts her head with his hand and looks deep into her eyes. "I don't want ya feeling sorry for me now. My life wasn't so bad." He lets go of her chin then looks out into the room. "I got all I needed from the sea or wouldn't have spent my life on the water. It's hard to describe. Sometimes, you feel like you're riding on the back of some giant monster. Other times, it's like skating on ice. I could spend hours looking at the heavens, counting those bits of light. There are voices in the wind and spirits in the fog. Some nights, I'd sing a song—maybe it was a prayer or a lonely man's wish." He looks off like he is imagining something.

"Could you sing it for me now?"

He laughs. "You don't want to hear my awful voice."

She touches his arm. "No, I do. You have a lovely speaking voice, and I'm sure your singing voice is wonderful too."

He begins humming, and a melancholy sound in Gaelic fills the room. It's magical and reminds her of the fairytale book about the sea. When he finishes, he looks over at her.

"That was lovely. What do the words mean?"

He sighs, wiping a slight wetness from his eyes. "Ah, it's about a sailor telling his love he misses her."

"I think I've heard that song before somewhere." She can't remember where, though.

"Of course you have." He turns to her. "I'm sure you've heard many songs on the water while drifting past boats at night. Probably heard our prayers, too. We're just a bunch of lovesick fools whittling away our time out there, dreaming of coming home to our women. Then once we're home, we can't wait to go to sea again."

Now is her opportunity. She reaches over and places her hand on top of Jason's. She feels a pang of sorrow for him, despite everything he has put her through.

"Jason, I'm dying inside being cooped up here. You've condemned me like I'm a horse waiting to be broken. Are you trying to break me? I don't understand why you're keeping me here."

He looks at her with sadness in his eyes. "Don't you want to be here with me?"

The urge to hug him is overwhelming. She isn't rejecting him as a person - only this whole messed up situation. Under different circumstances, they may have even been friends.

Being trapped here, she's learned he holds an admiration for the ocean, just as she does. So why can't he understand she is going crazy, with the water so close but unable to immerse herself in it? It's eating away at her soul. She needs her freedom back.

"I thought someday you'd come around, and we could..." He turns away, but there's a glimmer of tears in his gray eyes.

Her heart aches, chipping away at the negative feelings

she previously harbored toward him. He knows nothing real about her yet seems to genuinely want her near. She never told him anything - not her real name, about her family, her father's business, or why she was at the seal island the day he found her. She sighs. No need to burst his bubble just yet. That will happen once she finds a way to escape.

Chapter Twenty-Two

Alice

Alice sits, staring at the intruder. He is an Asian man in a suit and gelled black hair. Annoyed that this man is bold enough to walk around to the back deck, where she's sipping a cup of coffee.

"Morning Mrs. Monroe. I understand your daughter is missing," he says.

"Who are you?"

"Mr. Lei sent me to help find your daughter."

"Oh," Alice replies. Well, at least he isn't looking for money.

"I was wondering if you have any information that might help locate her."

She isn't going to tell him--a stranger. "I've hired a detective already," she snaps.

"May I ask who?" The man stares at her.

"Ben Stone. And I have no idea where Colleen is. If you want to know anything, talk to the police or Ben."

She gets up and goes inside, locking the door behind her. Pulling the curtains together, she peeks out the crack between them. The man walks around her deck, then to the stairs that lead to the beach, and looks down. She debates calling Detective Jackson, but after picking up her phone, her fingers punch in Ben's number.

"A man just showed up on my deck asking questions about the investigation," she tells him. "He said Mr. Lei sent him. I don't know if that's true, but I thought I would let you know. I'll ask Jody to call and find out. I don't know why Mr. Lei would send someone here."

Ben hummed. "Could you describe the man to me?"

"He's about six feet tall, heavyset, black hair. I'm pretty sure he is Asian—maybe even Chinese, but I've never been good at telling a Chinese person from all the other Asian countries, I'm afraid."

"Thank you for the information."

THERE IS a knock at the door. Jody walks over and opens it before Alice gets there. Detective Jackson stands in the doorway. Alice's eyes widen with concern at his presence.

"I thought I would stop by and see how you're doing."

Alice reaches around and jerks the door wide open. Jody gives her a disapproving look.

"Mrs. Monroe." He tips his head.

"Have you found Colleen?"

"No."

"Then why are you here?" Jody inquires, intensely staring at him.

"Have you noticed anything out of the ordinary lately?" Jackson asks.

"I heard footsteps the other night out on the driveway," Alice tells him.

Jody frowns at her. "It was a raccoon, Mother. Brian spotted it with his flashlight, remember?"

Alice grits her teeth, but Jackson starts talking again before she answers.

"I understand you reported suspicious characters on a boat to Ben Stone."

Her mind goes to the Asia man who showed up on her deck, wondering if he is one of the men she saw in the boat. "I did. Did you find out who they were?"

"No," Jackson replies. "But if any strangers approach you, either of you, don't hesitate to call me."

"Does this have anything to do with the notices Brian put up?" Alice asks.

"No… Although, someone may use the flyer as an excuse to get close to you, claiming to have information. Don't let them in. Refer them to the police. Offer to call me in front of them."

"But what if they found something?" Alice asks. She isn't going to close the door on someone who knows where her baby is.

"Let the police sort that out. We are more concerned about your safety."

Jody crosses her arms in front of her. "I don't understand."

He looks over at Jody, "Is it possible for your husband to stay with you?"

"I could call and ask, but is that necessary?"

"I don't want to sound sexist, but I'd feel better if you two ladies weren't staying here alone."

"Why? What's the problem?" Jody asks. "Are we in danger?"

Jackson purses his lips, then says, "With the flyers out, someone may come forward with a phony ransom note, looking for the money."

Alice turns to Jody. "See, I told you that was a bad idea."

"Just be on guard." Jackson nods.

"Thank you for stopping by." Jody closes the door.

Alice reaches for a cigarette off the kitchen counter and leans her back against the edge. "Well, what do you make of that?" she asks.

"I think he isn't telling us something," Jody replies.

"That's an understatement. With all these people working on finding Colleen, you'd think they would tell us something by now," Alice grumbles.

"I'll call Brian. I know he's busy, so I'm not sure he can come. I'm working in the other room and don't have access to the confidential stuff on the computers at the office. All I'm doing is answering emails and passing them on to other people, so I know Brian isn't going to want to come."

Alice rolls her eyes. "Then tell him to stay in Seattle. I certainly don't want him here—" Her sentence dissolves into coughs. She steadies herself on the counter as they rip through her lungs.

"Are you okay, Mom?"

Alice nods with her eyes closed. She just needs to get the cough under control.

Chapter Twenty-Three

Colleen

Jason motions her toward his boat. Colleen is unsure of what he wants her to do. Finally, he comes over and takes her hand, pulling her to the side.

"Get in." Jason points to the boat.

She looks over at him. "Why?"

"Just get in," he grumbles. "I'll explain later." Jason points to the front of the boat. She takes hold of the metal railing and steps onto the ladder bolted to the side. Once on board, she wades to the front of the boat, where the crane and pulley are mounted. In an open box, there are neatly coiled ropes, chains, and plastic ties. She looks up at Jason looming over her, his intentions suddenly unclear.

The area is crowded with round crab pots and wires the size of ropes. At the bottom, a few floats lay in a pile next to several chests.

Jason enters the boat's cab and starts the engine. He backs out and turns the boat toward the open water.

Colleen's heart pounds as Jason steers the boat away from the shore. Where is he taking her? She searches his face for any sign of his intentions, but his eyes reveal nothing.

He speeds through the waves, bouncing along.

Colleen grips the railing, her hair wildly blowing in the wind. She watches as the shore disappears behind them. The place where Jason held her captive is only a brown speck on a green hill.

There is a land mass to the south as they move farther out in the water. Next, boats in what appears to be a bay. She recognizes the land formation: it's Cook's Cove. She wasn't on some secluded island; Jason's place is along the coast to Bellingham. She could escape if she made her way to the main highway.

They head west for a while. Jason slows the boat as they approach the island where he first tried to capture her. He cuts the engine. Coming out of the cab, he goes to a box next to her and unlocks it. He points at it, lit from behind by sunlight, his shadow cast across the bow, and time stands still.

She blinks, trying to understand what he wants her to do.

"It's your skin. Put it on. I'm letting you go." He gestures with his arm to the open water.

She gets up and opens the lid of the box. Inside is her gray spotted wetsuit. Jason still believes she's a seal.

Standing there with her sea legs to keep her steady, she stares at him. This is not the way for her to escape. If she puts her suit on and swims to the island, she'll be stranded with no food and no way off. The island is an animal refuge. Though she went there, visitors were forbidden. She'd have a better chance of escaping from Jason's house now that she knows where it is.

Curious, she asks, "What changed your mind? Why do you want to let me go now?"

He looks out at the water and runs his hand down his beard. "It may be the curse of the story. I don't know. But Selkie, I can't do this anymore." He glances back at her. "I don't want to force you to stay with me if you don't want to. It's just not right." He sighs. "If you want to run off to the sea, then go. I'll not be stopping you. At least I've had the experience of your company and someone to lo—" His voice cracks, and he looks down. "Please forgive me for any harm I've caused you."

"Oh, Jason." She realizes his growing fondness for her. "No."

"No?" His eyes flash to her, and he stands back.

"This island isn't my home. I don't want you to leave me here." She points to the seals dotting the rocks.

He puts his hand on top of his head. "It's not? If you want to go somewhere else, tell me, and I'll take you there."

Colleen isn't ready to explain her situation to him. It's too complicated. "Please, take me back."

"I just told you. I can't keep you locked up in the shed anymore. You should go."

"I don't...want to." She swallows hard, trying to understand why her heart is twisting at the thought of leaving him.

"Selkie, what am I going to do with you?" He looks at the island, the wind ruffling the long hair below his knitted hat.

She closes the lid to the chest. "Take me back to your place. We'll figure something out."

"Well, I have some work to do first." He turns to the cabin.

"Okay," she says, chewing her lip and moving back to where she was sitting.

He drives the boat north until a coastline appears. The sunlight reveals ghostly winds on the water, dancing. She watches as birds skim the surface.

The roar of the engine soon stops. Jason comes out of the cab with an extra pair of rubber bibs and gloves. "As long as you're here, do you want to help me?"

It takes a moment for his words to register. He wants her help with the crab pots. "Sure." She wonders what that entails. But is willing to help, so she takes them from him. After climbing into the oversized rubber overalls and cinching them up so much there is no strap left, and the bib comes to just under her chin, she quickly braids her hair, tying the end with a piece of twine. She laughs at herself, thinking she looks like a giant yellow banana.

He opens an ice chest. "We're going to bait these crab pots and pull up the others." He takes out a package of chicken legs and tosses it to her. "Make a tasty treat for these greedy little buggers."

She stares at the raw meat. "What do you want me to do?"

"I'd like you to tie several of these legs together. Next, I'll have you put them on this little tray with a salmon head. We'll shove them in this pot here." He lifts the cage. "The crabs will come in this little opening but won't be able to get out." He moves the flap for her to see.

Colleen wraps twine around the legs with her bare

fingers, making a nice bow. Then she picks up the fish head, wrinkling up her nose, and puts everything in the tray like Jason showed her.

He smiles as he takes it from her and sets it in the cage. After attaching the crab line, he lowers it into the water and secures the float. He then powers up the boat, moving it until it's next to other floats in the water.

Jason guides the floats with a pole, then reaches down, attaching a cable, and uses a pulley to bring the pot up. A cage appears full of legs moving all around as the crabs climb on top of each other. Water gushes out the sides as he hoists the pot into the boat.

"Here're some gloves." He tosses her a pair. "Careful, you don't get pinched."

He opens the top of the cage and dumps the squirming things onto the boat floor.

"These are Dungeness crabs. We need to throw the females back." He picks one up and shows her how to tell the sex of the crab. "We also need to measure them. They must be 6.25 inches. Here's a gauge for measuring. Toss the ones that aren't that size."

As they work together, he hums a tune, looking over at her occasionally and smiling. She joins him as he repeats his song, trying to follow along. They do this until the pots are empty. After that, they place the remaining crabs inside another chest, and finally, Jason cranks the handle to bring up the anchor.

The sun is beginning to set, sending pink and orange spreading out across the sky on the horizon. The light reflects on Jason's mane, giving the illusion his deep mahogany is woven with flames. His eyes are like the glow from a lighthouse, setting their beam on her. She feels his spirit guiding her toward him.

He drops his eyes and goes to the controls. Colleen follows him inside the cab and stands next to him. "That was fun," she says, smiling up at him.

He puts an arm around her, hugging her to his side. "You did a great job. Thanks."

Leaning into him, she realizes she isn't afraid. It happened gradually. There's no defining moment when she understood he wasn't going to hurt her. She looks over at him. He isn't the monster she once thought; he is only a fisherman—a man she's grown to like, to care for. Maybe even have deep feelings for.

Soon, the temperature drops, and she puts on the heavy coat he offers her. Opening a thermos, he hands her a cup of warm broth. She takes a sip and hands it back to him. Together, they watch the stars come out. He points out the constellations to her, which she already knows, but lets him tell her anyway. He glances at her when he thinks she isn't looking. She smiles. For the first time in a long time, she's content, like she belongs somewhere, with someone.

When they reach the dock, Colleen jumps out and secures the ropes. Next, she helps Jason wheel the container of crabs to a large ice chest near the shed. Once they finish, Colleen steps out of the overalls and hands them back to Jason. Then she heads to the shed.

Jason hurries over. He takes the lock off and pockets it. "I—" His eyes search hers. "You're free to go when you want."

She smiles and nods. "Goodnight, Jason."

Inside, she washes her hands and arms in the sink. After a while, there is a knock at the door, and she opens it. A plate of food is sitting on the ground outside. She looks around, but Jason is gone.

As Colleen sits alone, eating her dinner for the first time since her release from the cage, her mind wanders, reflecting on the subtle ways Jason made her stay more pleasant. Today's boat excursion lingers in her thoughts; it was fun. She's always wanted to live on a boat, something Jason seems to share. Unlike the men she's dated, who prefer fair-weather sailing and quick trips back to shore, Jason understands the sea's rhythm. He appreciates not just skimming its surface but exploring the mysteries it holds.

She takes another bite of her sandwich. Did she really want to go back to her old life, fighting to be herself all the time with people who don't understand her?

Jason isn't a monster—a bit confused, that's all. She can't blame him for capturing her. He's lonely and wants to find someone to share his life with. Believing his only hope is in a silly myth.

As she crawls into bed that night, she wonders what it would be like to live without all the modern-day distractions. To be free to sail across the water into the sunset. Then she thinks about her mother. Gosh, her poor mother. What is she going to tell her?

———

THE FOLLOWING DAY, a note sits next to her breakfast.

Went to town for supplies. Hope to see you when I return. But if I don't, I wish you the best.

Freedom. She prayed for this moment, and now she can finally leave. She is no longer stuck living in this shed. Free to go outside. Colleen looks around the room, opens the door, and wanders into the yard, finding the gravel driveway. She follows it.

Colleen arrives at an asphalt-covered road, stops, and turns around. 'Do not enter' and 'No trespassing' signs are posted at the beginning of Jason's driveway.

A car rushes past. Colleen watches it disappear down the road. For so long, it's only been her and Jason. She sticks out her thumb when another car approaches. It slows and pulls over. But as she makes eye contact with the driver—an older man in a polo shirt, her excitement fades, and she waves him on.

She can't just leave without an explanation. She needs to tell Jason the truth. Besides, she has no idea what is waiting for her outside this place or how to deal with it.

Colleen turns around and walks down the path to the beach and sits on the rock where seals are sunning themselves. The ladies wave their heads in acknowledgment and bark.

"Hello," she greets them. "I don't have any fish for you today." She holds out the palms of her hands for them to see.

They continue coming closer, wiggling up onto the rocks near her. She thinks of them as friendly cats or dogs, just wanting her companionship.

As their large eyes look at her, she wonders what they are thinking. Did they come here for a reason other than curiosity?

She walks along the shore and spots a rock in the shape of a heart and picks it up.

"Selkie."

She turns. Behind her, Jason is standing on the trail.

He's holding a paper in his hand and his eyebrows furrow with concern.

"Is this you?" He points to the picture on the flier.

She approaches and takes it from him, and reads it. *'Missing person. Reward for information leading to the whereabouts of Colleen Monroe. Last seen on a sailboat in the water around the San Juan Islands. Please call...'*

She takes a deep breath and nods. *I guess now is the time to tell him.*

He turns, looking off into the trees. "So, you aren't a selkie?" His voice is cold. "You never were a selkie. You're this *Colleen* woman people are looking for."

She clasps her hands together nervously. "Yes. I am."

He bends over like he's in pain, then raises a fist to his mouth. "Oh, Christ. I've kidnapped a woman and kept her in my shed." He paces restlessly.

Colleen reaches out to him. "Jason, I—"

"I'll go to jail for this."

"Jason."

Suddenly, he stops, looking at her with wide eyes. "You should leave now!"

"Jason, I'm not going to tell them!"

His hands drop to his sides. "You're not?"

She shrugs. "No. I have no intention of getting you in trouble for what you did. You were confused. I should've explained things to you earlier."

"You must think I'm an idiot." He pulls off his hat, throwing it to the ground.

"Jason, I ran away, and you rescued me. Someone was chasing me. I think they wanted to hurt me. Who knows what might have happened to me if you hadn't come along."

He turns to face her. "Someone was chasing you? Why?"

She glances at the ground. "It's a long story, I don't quite understand myself."

He puts his finger under her chin so she will look him in the eyes. "Tell me."

Colleen swallows, then begins. "My father owned a shipping business. After he died, things got a little chaotic. My sister was trying to run the company because my mother didn't want the responsibility." She knows this doesn't make sense to Jason but continues, "One day, I went to the aquarium with my friend, Eric Lau. When we came out, two strange men were following us. Eric took off running. I don't know what happened to him. He disappeared. I was worried about him and went to Eric's place, but he wasn't there. Then, those same men started following me. I needed to hide, so I took my sailboat out on the water. I was scared. I wanted to figure out what to do. After that, you found me."

"I don't think I understand."

"Neither do I, but by staying with you, I've had time to think about my life." Colleen's words stick in her throat. "I've realized that—"

He interrupts her, "You need to go and tell the police so these men won't bother you anymore."

She shakes her head. "If I leave here, I can't go like this." She points to her dress. "I need decent clothes, or they'll wonder why I'm dressed in this outfit and suspect something." She looks at him. "We'll have to figure out a story to tell everyone so you don't get into trouble."

"What do you plan on telling these people?"

She chews her lip and thinks for a moment, turning over the rock in her hand. "That I've been staying with you. That you're my boyfriend?"

"Yeah, they'll never believe that. Look at me." Jason turns away and runs his hand over the top of his hair.

She replies to the back of his head, "Maybe after we both get some new clothes and fixed up a little...they'll believe it."

Jason kicks at the dirt. "You want me to pretend to be someone I'm not?"

Colleen let out a sigh. "Just for a little while."

"Oh, Selkie—I mean, Colleen. You're asking too much of me." He backs away from her. "I'm not a city person. I don't know how to act around those people."

"Please. I'll do all the talking. You can go back to who you are after this is over."

"I don't know about that."

"Promise me you'll think about it."

He scratches the side of his face through his beard. "All right, but don't expect me to change my mind."

"I guess we better move stuff around in case someone shows up here. I don't want anyone to know I've been staying in your shed."

"Right." He starts walking toward the building.

"Jason?"

"What?" He turns.

She holds out the rock. "I found this on the beach. It's for you."

He takes it from her. "It's a heart."

She blushes.

"Thanks." His face lights up. "I'll keep it as a reminder of you."

A sadness blows through her like a breeze across the water. She forces a smile. "I guess we better get busy."

In no time, the two of them hauled things around to make the shed appear like a storage area again.

"I suppose you'll be staying in me house now," he says, with a massive grin on his face.

"Yes, I guess so." She's unsure about this new living arrangement. "Tomorrow, we should go into Bellingham, though."

He opens the door for her and steps back.

She walks into a tiled entry that serves as a mudroom. Rows of boots are on the floor, and coats suspended on hooks along the wall. Farther inside is a modest, comfortable living room. A large stone fireplace in the middle of one wall. For seating, there's an overstuffed chair, a black leather recliner, and a worn couch with a blanket over the back. As her eyes travel the room, she notices pictures on the walls and goes over for a closer look. They are etchings of old sailboats.

She turns and smiles. "Do you like sailing?"

"I haven't done any, but I'd like to learn. 'Tis a dream of mine to sail to Hawaii someday. Don't know if it will ever happen or not."

"You should go. It would be a wonderful adventure." She sees the large oak bookcase and immediately heads to it, reading the titles of the books. She pulls out *The Old Man and the Sea* by Hemmingway. "This is one of my favorites."

He comes over to see what she's holding, then smiles. "Mine too."

Glancing around the room again, something's missing:

a TV. There is an old record player on a table and a stack of albums, but no fancy sound system or a radio.

"Do you have a computer somewhere?" she asks.

"No. Wouldn't know how to use one if I did."

"A cell phone?"

Jason shakes his head.

Wow, Jason lives in a place without all the chatter of the world.

"I've never had a guest before either, so I don't have another place for you to stay tonight. You can sleep in me bed, and I'll sleep on the couch."

"Oh no, Jason. That's nice of you, but I can sleep out here."

"You sure?"

She nods. "I don't want you to give up your bed for me."

"I better fix us something to eat, then. You hungry?"

She nods.

He heads for the kitchen while she sits on the couch and continues to look around. The place is small, but there is a homey feel to it. Some pillows and new curtains would do wonders to cheer it up.

She lays her head back. It's an actual living room with lamps and books to read. This is a comfortable hideaway. Her smile drops to a frown. She has no idea what to expect after leaving this place. Her old life feels so distant, artificial. She sniffs as tears push into her eyes. Why is returning so hard?

Chapter Twenty-Four

Ben

Ben's on his phone checking in with Mrs. Monroe while walking the back streets of Bellingham. He doesn't think Colleen is locked up in any buildings there, but he keeps getting strong vibrations of evil drifting around in the area like a serpent.

"Ben, every time I call that friend of yours, Detective Jackson, from the Bellingham police department, I get the run around from them. Do you know why?"

"They have other cases they are working on too." He stops and looks up at the telephone pole where seagulls are gathered.

"Are you telling me my missing daughter isn't a priority with them?"

"They need to balance their time." He isn't going to tell

her the truth. No mother wants to hear that the police aren't spending every waking moment on their case.

"What about you? You haven't told me anything, either. I have no idea what I'm paying you for. I'm starting to think I should hire someone else to find Colleen."

"These things take time. Remember, you hired me to explore all the possibilities."

"I'm just…."

"I understand. I want to reassure you that I'll have some answers soon."

"You can't tell me now?"

"I don't think that would be wise."

"All right, but I'm counting on you. So don't let me down."

Ben ends the call. He's not ready to mention his hunch about Colleen's disappearance being connected to her husband's death and Monroe Shipping. No need to give Mrs. Monroe more things to worry about.

Ben knows that if the Triad is involved, it changes everything. If they abducted Eric and Colleen, he could be in a race against time.

He calls his friend, Detective Jackson. "Hey, it's Ben. Got a minute? I need a huge favor…"

Ben explains what he discovered to Detective Jackson—Eric's secret relationship, the Triad coin, and Sam's suspicion of their involvement.

Jackson is concerned. "Hey buddy, you weren't hired to chase down what happened to Charles Monroe and Eric—what's his name? Keep focused on the Monroe girl. Let the big guns worry about international crime."

"I understand. But I believe there's a connection."

"I know you're bullheaded. But Ben, tread carefully. If

Taken from the Sea

the Triad are behind this, they won't appreciate your nosing around," Jackson warns him.

"I know, I know," Ben replies, "I just wanted to give you a heads up if I need some backup."

"Hey, Ben. You know I will. Just be careful."

"Right."

He could smell pizza, and his stomach growled. The thought of a combo slice made his mouth water.

As Ben rounds the corner, he looks up to find two Asian men heading in his direction, with their eyes intently focused on him. A chill travels down his back. Aren't these the same guys he ran into before?

He better find out if they are interested in him or just doing a stare-down.

He spins and dashes down the nearest alley, feet pounding the pavement. Shouts echoing behind as they give chase.

But he has the advantage of knowing every inch of this town and where to hide. He zigzags down the different streets, ducking behind bushes and fences as they run past him. They're apparently good at figuring out his maneuvers because soon they are back on his trail.

He escapes down a back alley, climbs on top of a closed garbage bin, and jumps over a wall. He veers to the left, where a homeless man is camped. Putting a finger to his mouth to indicate his secret, Ben tosses his hat into an open dumpster, grabs a blanket from the man, squats, wraps the filthy thing around him, and lowers his head.

The men following him trot past and keep going. Sitting there, Ben runs an escape route through his mind.

Climbing into the dumpster, he retrieves his hat. Fortunately, it isn't soiled. Ben's mind races. He needs to lose them quickly before they catch on to his tricks. Spying a fire escape, he leaps and pulls down the ladder, scurrying up to the roof.

Reaching the top, he gets his bearings. An office building next door is his best bet. Ben backs up, and takes a running leap, barely clearing the gap between roofs. No time to look back. He has to keep moving. He flies across the rooftops, vaulting air units and ducts, until he finds a safe place to rest.

From his coat pocket, he pulls out a small pair of binoculars. *Where should I look?*

He calls for his bird spirit. It spins into the air like a swirl of smoke, stretches its wings, flying above the buildings. Focusing on a nearby street, it lets out a screech.

Ben swings his binoculars in that direction and watches the men backtrack. Finally, they give up. His bird spirit follows and watches them disappear into a warehouse along the water. It then returns to Ben.

If he was to guess, someone told those men he's looking for Colleen and they're counting on him to provide information they don't have. They'll use force to get it from him. These thugs narrowed their search to Bellingham, expecting her to show up here. But when? Hours, days?

He and his spirit will be waiting, watching for signs. He needs to get to her first. Colleen's life depends on it.

Chapter Twenty-Five

Colleen

Jason drives the boat to the marina in Bellingham and moors it at the guest dock. Colleen pulls down the hat he gave her and wraps herself in his bulky coat, trying to hide her looks.

"Here's some money. Buy yourself a pretty dress and whatever else you want. I'll meet you back at the dock at four o'clock." He shoves a wad of hundred-dollar bills in her hand, then helps her climb out of the boat.

Colleen quickly purchases a prepaid wireless phone so she can call her mother once she's ready. Next, she needs a decent outfit.

As soon as she walks into the department store, she feels the eyes of other customers on her. She looks like a homeless person in her oversized coat. Letting out her breath, she strolls the aisles, hoping no one recognizes her.

Her first stop is for a pair of shoes. She goes to the sales rack, where shoes are on display according to size. Jason gave her a couple of socks to wear to cover her bare feet, and she isn't prepared to deal with a salesman who'd see her webs, so she picks out several pairs of boots and tries them on by herself, finally deciding on a black pair.

She rides the escalator to the lingerie department and buys some decent underwear and a bra. Jeans and sweaters are next on her list. After making her purchases, she goes to the ladies' room, pulls off the tags, and slips on a pair of jeans, the boots, and a tight-fitting blue sweater, depositing her dress in the garbage on the way out. Picking up her shopping bags again, she walks around the store, still wearing the oversized coat and cap.

While going through the rack containing an assortment of coats and jackets, she notices a man staring at her from across the room. Wondering if he's a store security guard or someone she should be afraid of she quickly takes a couple of coats to the dressing room. Glancing around when she comes out, Colleen hurries to the checkout counter to pay for a coat.

Outside on the street, her stomach churns with anxiety. There are only a few people walking around. Still, someone might be lurking in the background, watching her..

Dressed in her new clothes, she hurries back to the boat with the rest of her packages, storing them on board. She folds Jason's coat and hat, setting them on his chair beside the controls. She wonders what his reaction will be when he sees her in her new outfit.

Returning to town, she finds a salon and gets a trim then her nails and makeup done. Looking in the mirror with her hair fixed and wearing new clothes, she looks like her old self again. But inside, she is a different person from the one that disappeared a while ago. After paying the bill, she slips on her new stylish coat and steps outside.

There's that feeling again nipping at her. She glances around to make sure she isn't being followed. Jason showed her a poster with her face on it, so she is vulnerable to being discovered. Their plan might work if she can sneak out of town and go back with Jason. From his place, they'll go to her house in Cook's Cove, and she'll introduce him as her boyfriend.

She passes a coffee stand and hesitates, then purchases a fancy coffee for Jason. She smiles. He's probably never tasted one before.

When she arrives at the slot where the boat is, she looks around, but Jason isn't waiting for her. Glancing at her new watch, it's five minutes before four. Suddenly, she is ashamed of herself. It's too much to expect of him to go along with her charade. It's wrong of her to ask him. Besides, Jason doesn't want to do this. She's acting selfish, just like her sister always accuses her of. Guilty of not thinking things through.

Colleen slumps her shoulders. It's questionable that anyone would believe their lie, anyway. It's a dumb idea. She needs to make up a different story about her disappearance. Check into a hotel here in Bellingham. That way, Jason won't be a part of the story she'd fabricate. He'd be free to go back to his life. No one will know the truth about where she's been all this time.

She glances around. She needs to leave before Jason arrives.

Colleen climbs aboard the boat and puts the coffee next to the controls in a cup holder. Next, she starts pulling out her packages setting them on the dock. Taking her new phone out of her purse, she quickly punches in her pickup location for a Lyft. Now that she has access to all her information, she might as well use it. Gathering her bags and walking toward the street, trying to manage her purchases, she hears Jason's voice call to her.

"Hey. Where are you going?"

She is afraid to turn around. She can't look him in the eyes; it's too painful to say goodbye. She tries running, but one of her bags splits, and clothes spill out on the dock.

"Selkie?"

Crouching down, she begins to cry. She covers her eyes as she hears the echo of his cane approaching.

"Hey, what's going on?"

Without looking up, she says, "Jason, this is my mess. I need to deal with it alone. You should go back home."

"Is that what you want? For me to leave you here?"

Tears drip down her face. When she looks up, mascara stings her eyes, so she looks down again. "Yes," she mutters.

"Okay then."

She hears him walk away.

Colleen pulls herself to her feet, wiping her eyes. Glancing over to where Jason's fishing boat is waiting, she brings her hand to her mouth.

There, approaching the boat is a handsome stranger. Gone is the wild hair, the unkempt beard. A gorgeous man wearing slacks, a tailored shirt, and a leather jacket is walking with a cane toward the boat. Is that Jason?

She's awestruck by the sight of him. Why in the world

did he ever think he's ugly? Jason is one of the most handsome men she's ever laid eyes on.

She swallows hard as his boat pulls out, leaving her behind. Tears run down her cheeks, and she wipes them away with the back of her hand once again. Then she stuffs the loose clothing into another bag and goes to the street. When the Lyft arrives, she gets in, and they drive off.

Chapter Twenty-Six

Colleen

Colleen sits on the bed in her hotel room, staring at her phone. Who should she call first? Her mother or Jody? Maybe she should call the police.

She decides on Jody.

"Where the hell have you been? Mother has been worried sick about you. I'm in the car, headed to Bellingham right now. Are you someplace close?"

The story Colleen prepared flew out of her mind. "Yes, I'm in Bellingham at the Northshore Hotel."

"I'll be right over to get you. You better have a reason for disappearing. Everyone's been looking for you."

There's a knock at the door.

"I'll call you right back," Colleen tells her.

"Shit," Jody hisses. "Don't hang up!"

"Tell Mother I'm safe." Colleen ends the call. Taking a

deep breath, she opens the door a sliver, expecting it to be someone from the hotel.

Her heart races as questions flood through her mind and words tangle in her mouth. The only ones she can push out are, "Eric. Oh my God."

He steps closer, nudging the door open, and throws his arms around her, hugging her in a tight embrace. After a moment, she pulls back, letting him inside her room, and closes the door.

"I thought you were dead!" Colleen says, still in shock at seeing him again.

"I'm glad I found you." He kisses her cheek.

She steps back, glaring at him. "What happened to you? I tried calling. I even went to your apartment looking for you. I was worried sick. I thought those men—"

He looks over to the window. "I've been hiding."

"So have I," Colleen adds. "I was going to turn myself in."

"Does anyone know you're here?" He asks, sounding urgent.

She hesitates. *Should she tell him she spoke to her sister?* "No."

He goes to the window, pulls the curtain back, and looks up and down the street below. "It isn't safe here. Follow me." He heads toward the door.

"I just got here." She protests, looking at the clothes still in their shopping bags on the floor.

He turns. "Bring your stuff. We need to get out of here. Quickly, before they find us."

"Who? Are we still in danger?" Was it a mistake for her to reappear without notifying the police first? She's so confused.

"If we don't leave this place soon, we will be. Did you

use a credit card and your real name when you checked in?"

"Not a credit card, but my real name."

He fishes out some cash from his pocket and hands it to her. "Tell them you were meeting a man here and needed discretion. You lied about your name and give them an extra fifty dollars to forget you were here."

Confused, she nods, her mind racing as she follows his lead. Her instincts scream that something's not right, but the urgency in Eric's voice is enough to propel her into action. So, she grabs her bags and leaves.

Eric is waiting in a car when she steps out of the hotel. Colleen climbs into the passenger's side, and they drive off.

She turns to him. "What's going on? Why are those men looking for us?"

"I'll tell you once we're someplace safe."

Her nerves are on edge again. She thought all of this was over, but now she's afraid they are both in danger again.

They didn't go far, stopping in a commercial area along the water. Eric gets out of the car, glances left and right, then motions to her, and they hurry over to a warehouse. He unlocks a door, disappearing inside. She follows him. It's dark in the warehouse, except for an opening in the back. He points to a door along a wall.

"Why are we here? Is this where you've been staying?" she asks as he unlocks the door, swinging it open for her to go inside. Colleen faces him after setting down her bags. "How did you know where to find me?"

He smiles. "I've been hiding in this building. I thought you might be in the area. I've been waiting for you to show up."

"How did you know I'd come to Bellingham?"

"You told me about your parent's house in Cook's Cove and how you like to sail out to the islands, so I thought this would be a logical place to look for you."

"Oh, right," Colleen recalls their conversation at the aquarium. "How did you know I was at the hotel?"

"I spotted you getting into a car near the marina and followed you."

"Oh." That's a strange coincidence. But this whole situation makes little sense. She looks around the room; it's an office. A desk with a computer sits along a wall. She moves closer to it. On the screen is a display of various camera feeds watching the marina. She gives Eric a quizzical look.

"I've been watching outside to make sure I was safe here. That's how I spotted you," he says.

There is an adjoining door. Curious, Colleen walks over, opens it, and looks inside. Sitting at a table are two men, both Asian. One's wearing black-framed glasses. She recognizes them as they scoot back their chairs jumping to their feet. These are the men who were chasing Eric outside the aquarium. Colleen does a quick about-face and slams into Eric's chest.

"Eric, we need to get out of here. These are the same men—"

He holds on to her tight. "Correct, and you aren't going anywhere."

"I don't understand." She tries pushing him away, but he isn't letting her go. "I thought those men were after you. That was the reason you were hiding."

"Yes, that's what I wanted you to believe."

"I was afraid when those men came after me. That's

why I left on my boat—to get away from them. I don't understand. So, no one was after you? Why did you deceive me? I thought we were friends."

"Sorry to disappoint you." He touches her face gently. "I warned you this might happen. But, unfortunately, you weren't willing to sell your shares in your father's business. So, without your cooperation, we had to resort to other methods to gain control of Monroe Shipping. And you are just another unfortunate casualty."

"But I don't have anything to do with the business. Jody's the one who works there."

He drags his finger across her cheek while she glares at him. "She's next on the list. First your father, then you—then her."

"My father? He died of a heart attack."

"Yes, that's what we wanted everyone to believe. His death was easy. We just switched his pills. But my friend, you were more difficult to get rid of than we thought. I needed you to take your boat out so no one would suspect what we were up to. I told the guys where to find you so we could make sure you drowned out there.

"Unfortunately, things didn't go as planned. They watched you go overboard. We weren't sure what happened to you after that because you took off the necklace I gave you, and then there was no way of tracking you. And I have no idea what happened to your phone."

She is pissed. How can he be so heartless? Killing her father and tracking her while she is out of her mind, worrying about him? Boy, he fooled her. All he cares about is gaining access to her father's business.

He squeezes his fingers together, choking her. Her hands go up, and she tugs at his so she can breathe.

"At first, we suspected someone rescued you but didn't know who. We thought you'd show up on one of the islands, but when you didn't, we realized you might have gone into hiding.

"There are posters all over town. Lucky for us, no one else knows you didn't drown. So now we'll take you for a ride on the water and drop you in for a swim to make sure you do this time."

Gasping for breath, she asks, "Are you going to kill my mother and Jody?"

"Your sister and her husband's death will result from an unfortunate accident next month while visiting Hong Kong on business. And your mother—the death of both daughters after losing her husband will push her over the edge. If the shock doesn't kill her, she'll be declared incompetent to run the business and, without heirs, forced to relinquish control."

"You bastard." She brings her knee up, slamming it into his balls.

"Ahhh," he bents over in pain.

Colleen bolts for the door, but one man grabs her arm before she can escape.

The other man slips a cloth over her mouth. After securing it, he smiles and looks over at Eric. "Since we plan to kill her anyway, can I have fun with her first?"

She freezes, not knowing what he plans to do next.

"She was wearing a wetsuit in the water, wasn't she?" he asked.

Colleen gulps.

The man wearing glasses replies, "I don't recall, but she wasn't wearing these clothes." He laughs. "Maybe we should help her out of them."

Furrowing her brows in horror, she glares at Eric.

Eric shakes his head and then places his hand on the shoulder of the man wearing the glasses. "Hey, we don't have time for you two to mess with her here. And I don't want anyone to see us carrying a body out of here. Let's get her on the boat and over to the islands. After that, you can take turns playing with her before you drop her in the water." Eric gestures to the door. "Now, let's get the boat ready and get the hell out of here."

The men drop their hands, and Colleen takes off, but Eric grabs her hair, yanking it. "Not so fast. You're not getting away this time."

One of the thugs pulls out a gun, pointing it directly at her. "I don't want to shoot you here because of the mess. But if you want to die with a hole in your head, then go ahead and try to escape."

Chapter Twenty-Seven

Ben

Earlier

Ben's crow spirit circles above the wharf and lands on a light post. Turning its head, the spirit bird focuses one eye on the heartbroken girl below as she sits on the dock with clothes scattered around her. It lets out a loud caw, then flies back into the heart of its master. Ben opens his eyes and begins setting his plan in motion. He hurries to the place where Colleen is crawling into the car.

I found Colleen. She's alive. He types into his phone. **I spotted her on the visitor's dock. She was using a cell phone, so she's set up a new account. I've included a photo of the license plate of the car she left in. Find out where she went and let me know. I don't know how much time we have. I believe she's in danger. There are a couple of thugs looking for her.**

He hits send, praying Jackson gets the message and

takes action immediately. Ben walks over to his car, ignoring an incoming call.

Ben wants to know who brought Colleen to the marina and looks up the name and numbers on his phone of the boat he saw her leaving from. He scrolls through the different listings. Finally, he discovers the boat's registered as a commercial vessel to Jason MacGregor, who lives in Cook's Cove. Once he recognizes the owner's address, the puzzle starts to come together. It confirms his suspicion that Ms. Monroe has been hiding in the area all along. Now he just needs to talk to MacGregor and find out the rest of the story.

He checks the missed call and discovers it's from Jody, so he listens to it.

"Hi, this is Jody Monroe. I thought you'd like to know that Colleen just called me, and I'm on the way there now. She's at the Northshore Hotel in Bellingham."

Ben quickly sends off a text of Colleen's location to Jackson, then debates going to the hotel but figures Jackson's got it covered, so he decides to find out where Colleen's been hiding instead, adding to his text. **I'll get back to you. I'm following another lead.**

Ben closes his eyes again, summoning his bird spirit. He needs to know where MacGregor's boat is going.

The bird soars above the marina and heads out to the open water. In his mind's eye, he can see the fishing vessel heading south along the coast back to Cook's Cove. The bird loops in the air and returns to where Ben stands.

Ben starts his car and races off, traveling well over the speed limit. He turns off the main highway at the 'No Trespassing' sign and travels down the gravel road toward the water. About a quarter mile in, he finds a man with a gun. The guy is tall and muscular, with a good-looking face. It's the same man he spotted departing on the fishing boat. A cane leans against one of the man's legs.

"This is private property, so you better turn around."

Ben kills the engine and gets out. He puts his hands up. "Are you Jason MacGregor?" he asks, walking toward the guy.

The man doesn't answer.

"I've come to ask you a few questions about Colleen Monroe," Ben says.

MacGregor raises the gun. "I said, this is private property, and if you don't have a warrant, you better leave."

"I'm a private investigator. Colleen's mother hired me to find her. I just want to ask you a few questions," Ben tells him.

"The woman you're looking for is not here."

"Yes, I know." Ben's phone buzzes. "I've got to answer this." Ben slowly reaches into his coat pocket, pulls out the phone, and holds it up, showing the guy it isn't a weapon.

"Colleen's gone. We traced her to a hotel, but she didn't stay long," Jackson says. "Her sister was there, though."

"Do you have any idea where she went?" Ben looks over at MacGregor, wondering what he knows.

"She left with a guy. But here's a twist—the receptionist could identify the man Colleen was with because he had come by earlier inquiring about a girl that fit Colleen's description. He is a tall, good-looking Asian man. Jody told me that might be Eric Lau. I'm a bit confused now. Do you think they've been hiding together?"

"Well, that's interesting. Can you track the car she left in? I'm worried that she may be walking into a trap."

"A trap?"

"Yes. I think this Lau guy is connected to the Triad, and that's why Colleen went into hiding."

"You better be right. But I must warn you, it'll take a few minutes before we can get there, something's come up and we're shorthanded right now. So if you can detain him until then, I'd appreciate it."

"Thanks. I'm heading back." Ben ends the call and slides the phone back into his pocket. He looks over at Jason again. "I'm aware you and Colleen know each other. She was crying when she got into a car and left. I suspect she wasn't happy to leave you."

"It was her choice," Jason replies.

Ben suspects their relationship is more than casual and says, "I don't know what was going on between you two, but if you care about her safety, you might want to hop in and come with me. I think she's in danger, and I have some questions that need answering."

"Why should I believe you?" Jason asks.

"Because I'm interested in discovering why she ran away. I think it has something to do with her father's business, and you might be able to tell me the details."

"You could be one of the men who wants to harm her. So why should I trust you?"

"Because I am Ben Stone, and I swear I'm telling you the truth." Ben places his hand on his heart. "And if you care for her, you better come with me now."

Jason scratches the side of his face, eyeing him. "So, you're that shaman I heard about?"

Ben nods.

Jason shrugs his shoulders. "You better not be lying to me." He lowers his gun.

"If we don't hurry, she just might disappear for good.

However, I'd prefer it if you didn't bring that weapon with you." He doesn't want to be responsible for Jason shooting someone if they encounter any trouble.

Jason stands there for a moment, leaves for his garage and returns without the firearm.

As they start traveling up the long driveway, Ben asks, "Has Colleen been staying with you this whole time?"

Jason just stares out the window.

"Are you two in a romantic relationship?"

Jason didn't answer the question, but Ben's gut tells him they care for each other—to what degree, he isn't sure, but he'll find out soon enough.

Ben's phone rings, and he puts it on speaker as he turns down the back road to the industrial area.

"We got the license plate off the video at the hotel and traced it on a surveillance camera to a parking lot outside a warehouse on the waterfront."

"Great. I'm already there."

"We'll catch up with you as soon as we can."

As they pull into the parking lot, Ben looks over at Jason. "You should stay here while I go in and check on things." He's uncomfortable about going in alone, but he can't wait.

Jason gets out. "I'm coming with you."

Ben looks over at Jason's cane. He has no idea if Jason will be an asset or a burden. Now he's questioning why he brought the guy along. "I guess it's just you and me, Jason, until the police arrive."

They head to the entrance. Ben glances around. "Why don't we split up? If you see something, text me." Ben brings out his phone.

"I don't own a phone." Jason tells him.

Who doesn't own a phone these days? "Okay, make a noise. Yell." He puts the phone back into his pocket. "You go around back, okay?"

Jason walks off, leaning on his cane.

Inside it's dark, except for a light from a door in the back that opens to the water. As Ben walks along, he spots an office off to the side. He quietly slips over and pushes open the door. It's empty.

When he comes out, he hears voices. There are several men outside the opening. Ben creeps along the wall of the building, stooping low, and peers around the edge.

A man is pointing a gun at Colleen's back and her mouth is gagged. Ben watches as another man pushes her along toward a boat. He needs to distract them.

Looking around, he finds an empty bucket on the floor and sends it flying against a wall near the opening. It makes enough noise to create interest. One man comes inside as Ben reaches into his holster under his coat and withdraws his gun. The man is tall, good-looking, and Asian. Ben's gut tells him it's Eric Lau.

Eric spots him. "We've got company!"

One man shoves Colleen forward as they enter the building. The gun-wielding man follows, his aim alternating between Ben and Colleen.

Ben focuses his gun on Eric. "Let her go."

A flurry of movement comes from the opening as Jason charges through and smacks the man nearest Colleen with his cane. The guy turns, and Jason jabs him in the stomach, causing the man to fall to his knees. Then, lifting his cane, he smacks it over the man's head with such force that it sends the guy to the ground in a thud, knocking him out.

Colleen pulls a gag rag down from her mouth. "Jason!" Ben hears the panic in Colleen's voice.

"Just shoot her!" Eric yells to the man holding the gun. "I want her dead. Then we'll deal with the others."

Jason looks over at Colleen. The gunman alternates his aim between Colleen, Jason, and Ben.

"Don't pay attention to the cripple," Eric shouts. "Shoot her. Now!"

"Make a move, and I'll shoot your boss," Ben's, ready to pull the trigger.

"Lau isn't my boss." The man laughs, glances over at Jason, then focuses his attention back on Colleen. A second before he squeezes the trigger, Jason flings himself at her. A shot rings out. Colleen's scream pierces the air.

Eric takes off running, but Ben shoots him in the thigh, and he drops to the floor. The other man turns his aim to Ben, and fires, but misses. Just then, Jackson and two officers come in through the back of the building, guns drawn. One officer apprehends Eric, while the other pursues the gunman, who trips and loses his weapon. They handcuff the thug before he can escape.

Colleen sits on the floor with Jason's head in her lap as blood from his chest pools around her. "I'm sorry. I'm so sorry, Jason. This is my fault. Please, don't die," she cries.

Chapter Twenty-Eight

Colleen

"You can go in now, Ms. Monroe."

Colleen gets up from her chair and goes to Jason's room. It's hard to believe that the man before her is the same person who was holding her captive in his shed. With his beard gone and his hair short, he looks like a completely different person. He has a strong jaw, clean-shaven cheeks, a dimple in his chin, and the hint of a smile crinkling the skin around his gray eyes. He's drop-dead gorgeous, in her opinion. If he only knew that with a shave and a haircut, women would be throwing themselves at him.

But then she smiles. Jason isn't like other men; he's a man of the sea and will never be content with an ordinary life on land with just any woman.

Jason turns his head on the pillow to face her. "Selkie,"

he whispers. His chest is bandaged, and wires are monitoring his heartbeat.

She bends over him. "I was so worried about you. I was afraid they'd killed you."

"Ah, if they had, it wouldn't be a bad way to go. Protecting you," he replies softly.

Tears roll down her cheek. "You silly man." She kisses him on the forehead.

He reaches for her hand and squeezes it.

Just then, a nurse sticks her head in the doorway. "Ms. Monroe, your mother is here."

Colleen bites her lower lip. She's been dreading this moment. Straightening up, giving Jason one last look, she waves and goes out the door.

Her mother immediately rises when Colleen enters the waiting room. Jody is there but remains in her chair, to stay out of the way, no doubt.

"Where in God's name have you been? I've been a wreck worrying about you!" Her mother glares.

"I..." She is still aching from seeing Jason. She wants to be with him, not making excuses for her disappearance.

Her mother's arms shoot out, grabbing Colleen and pulling her tightly to her chest. "I've had people looking for you everywhere." She lets go, wiping a tear from her cheek. "Where have you been, sweetheart?"

"Ah..." What can she say that won't sound incriminating?

"Jody told me you called her. She went to the hotel, and you'd checked out by the time she got there. It was Ben who let me know I'd find you here." Bringing up a tissue, she coughs and wipes her mouth. "He said the police rescued you from men who wanted to harm you. Why would they want to do that?"

Colleen is still trying to make sense of what happened herself. Jody's listening to their conversation. At least she has the courtesy not to add her two cents.

"I don't know," Colleen finally says.

"Were those men holding you captive? Did they hurt you?" Her mother's eyes searched her face for answers.

"No. I was safe until Eric showed up at my hotel room."

"If you were safe all this time, why didn't you call me?" Her mother asks in a loving voice, running her hand down Colleen's hair.

"I was going to." Colleen looks back as a nurse steps down the hall to Jason's room. She wants to leave and check to see if he's okay.

"You should've asked someone to bring you to the house in Cook's Cove once you finished with the police. What on earth are you doing here at the hospital?"

"I came to see the man who saved my life to make sure he was okay," Colleen replies. "He's my…boyfriend, Jason." Her mother isn't going to like hearing this. "I've been staying with him at his house on the coast." Colleen watches to see if her mother believes her.

Alice's demeanor changes. She frowns, then through gritted teeth, says, "You abandoned your damn boat to go off with some man? Please. You expect me to believe that? You could have gone back and brought your boat to the marina and spent time with him. This makes no sense to me. And if you were safe, why the hell didn't you tell anyone where you were? I was worried sick that you drowned out there."

"I…" She doesn't have an answer. Raising her voice in

frustration. "I couldn't!" She's exhausted from all she'd been through. Why can't her mother give it a rest just this once?

"Shush." Her mother arches her brows, then whispers, "Did you really think people would believe a daughter of mine would be with such a man when you concocted this lie? I don't know what game you're playing, but it ends now."

"I've been hiding at Jason's for a reason."

"And what reason is that?" Alice coughs into a tissue again.

Colleen notices the trace of red. "It's a long story."

"Well, start talking."

Colleen let out a sigh. "After Eric Lau disappeared, I didn't know where to go. I didn't feel safe in Seattle."

"If you didn't feel safe, you should have called me," her mother reaches out, touching Colleen's arm. "I would have notified the police."

Looking down, Colleen replies, "I just wanted to get away. I was afraid. While out on my boat, I ran out of gas and there was no wind. I thought someone out there was after me, so I jumped overboard. Jason pulled me from the water, and I left with him. He's been protecting me all this time." Avoiding her mother's eyes Colleen continues, "While I was staying with him, we developed feelings for each other." This wasn't quite the same story Colleen told the police. When they asked for her statement, she told them Jason and her were only friends.

"That stranger?" I don't believe you. Alice says in a clipped tone. "That fisherman isn't good enough for you."

Colleen clenches her jaw. "Why does that matter?"

"You're a Monroe. We have a certain... image.

Besides, he isn't the type of man you normally spend time with, and you know that. Why didn't you call me if he wasn't forcing you to stay with him? I could have sent someone out to get you. I bet he was after your money all along."

"If you believe that, why didn't he ever ask for any?"

"Perhaps he was waiting for the right time. Maybe now he wants the reward that was offered. Who knows what goes on in the minds of people like him?"

"That's cold of you." Colleen balls her fists. "He's not that kind of man, Mother."

A beat of silence stretches between them. Alice's face crumples, and for a fleeting moment, Colleen glimpses a vulnerability as fragile as breaking glass.

"I just want what's best for you, sweetheart." Alice says softly.

Colleen sighs. "Why can't you see the best for me is with Jason?"

"Hmm. I don't understand why you're protecting him," she croaks, then suppresses a cough. "I bet there's more you aren't telling me."

"Please. I don't want him to get hurt over the trouble I put you through."

"I think you're lying about him."

"Damn it, Mother! You don't know anything. Look at me. I'm fine. I chose to stay with him, so leave Jason out of it." Colleen is clenching her teeth, biting back the rage she's experiencing over her mother's accusations. "I can make my own decisions about who I want to be with. I don't need your approval. Just butt out of my life!"

"Oh, you think you're so smart, do you? While waiting here, I looked into who Jason MacGregor is, so don't keep lying to me, Colleen. This man you claim to have been staying with is a filthy fisherman."

She put her hands on her hips, glaring at her mother. Tossing one arm in the air, she declares, "Yes, he is a fisherman. But I care for him deeply. I was staying with him because I was afraid of the men who were chasing me. Please, Mother, leave Jason out of this." Her heart's racing.

"You'll have to promise me you'll return to Seattle and never see this man again. If you don't, I will have him investigated, and if he has so much as an unpaid parking ticket, I'll see that he's punished for it."

"I..." Colleen digs her nails into her palms. *Oh God, what if they learned the truth?* She has no other choice. It's the only way to keep Jason from being investigated. He'd probably tell them what he did, and they'd send him to jail for kidnapping her. She can't let that happen. "I'll go back to Seattle." She lets out an angry breath.

Colleen glances up, spotting the same Native American man coming through the door who rescued her. He walks over to join them.

"I'd like to talk to you privately, Ms. Monroe, if that's okay." He looks over at Alice, and she nods. Colleen follows Ben outside to a garden area, where she takes a seat on a bench.

"As you know, I've been working on this case. Your mother hired me to find you," Ben reminds her.

The sun behind him silhouettes his hat, giving it the appearance of a beak. His arms are bent, resting on his hips. For a moment, the image of a bird—a crow—flashes through Colleen's mind.

She raises her hand to shade the sun and asks, "Is Jason going to be arrested? Is that what you're going to tell me?

Did he say something? I told the police that Jason and I were friends. I was staying with him because I was afraid. He has nothing to do with Eric Lau and those awful men. The police have no reason to think he's done anything wrong." She fights the tears filling her eyes, then breaks down. "I just promised Mother I would never see him again if she didn't go after him." Colleen brings her hands to her face, hiding her grief.

"Is that what you want? To never see him again?" Ben asks.

Colleen swipes at the tears pricking her eyes. Her lips quiver. She can't answer.

"From what I've observed, something is going on between the two of you, and it's more than just friendship. Jason took a bullet for you."

"I know, and I feel terrible. And now Mother's expecting me to do the impossible. She wants me to fulfill my father's dream. But I don't want to go back and live that life. I'm not cut out to work at Monroe Shipping." She sniffs.

"You haven't given her a good enough reason for why you left your boat in the middle of the water. She knows how important it is to you and finds it odd that you would abandon it and go off with a stranger."

Colleen rubs her forehead. It's all getting to be too much; she wants tell the truth. To be rid of the burden of all the lies.

"Since no one could get anything out of Jason about his involvement, you need to tell me what happened," Ben whispers, "I'll do my best to protect both of you."

Colleen sighs. "Okay. If I tell you the truth, promise me you won't hold it against Jason."

"I promise."

She bites her lip. "I know you're going to think this is weird, but when Jason found me in the water, he thought I was some mystical creature. So, he brought me back to his place to live."

"A selkie, perhaps?"

Colleen cocks her head. "How did you know?"

"I know about your webbed feet and am familiar with many legends and myths. Cook's Cove is rich with unexplainable events."

"I don't blame him for what he did. He was just lonely, that's all."

"I know the story of the fisherman and the selkie."

Her eyes flash to him. "So, you understand why he… rescued me?"

Ben nods his head.

"Please don't let them arrest him. He's a good man. I swear to God, he never hurt me."

Ben reaches over and places his hand on her arm. "I believe you. I'll do my best to deter them. I'm just glad you weren't captured and killed by the men looking for you."

Chapter Twenty-Nine

Colleen

Once finding the flash drive she took from her dad's file cabinet, Colleen turns it over to the police to make sense of. As she hands the small device to Detective Morris of the Seattle Police Department, her stomach knots. She's hoping the drive contains the evidence they need to finally unravel the truth behind her father's murder.

The police assure Colleen they will uncover the truth, but they are still working out the details, so they ask her to keep quiet until they have a strong case against those involved.

Every time she thinks of Eric fury rises inside over his betrayal. She thought he cared for her, but he didn't. He was just using her. Biting her tongue to hold back angry tears, she hopes Eric rots in jail for the role he played in her father's suspicious death.

When she returns to the shipping office, people stare at her, whispering as she strolls past. Hiding with the door closed, spending her days looking through papers Colleen doesn't understand, is her daily routine. Now that Jody is aware of the plot to kill them both, she is more determined than ever to do an outstanding job of running Monroe Shipping. So, Colleen lets Jody control things and stays out of her way.

Colleen keeps her end of the bargain by showing up, but she resents it and refuses to talk to her mother.

LATE ONE NIGHT while watching TV, Colleen's phone buzzes. Picking it up, she notices it's from her mother's maid.

"Colleen, your mother was coughing so much she couldn't breathe, so I called 911. They rushed her to the hospital."

"Thank you for letting me know." She brings her hand to her mouth, feeling guilty for not speaking to her mother after returning to Seattle.

Panicked by the news, Colleen quickly calls her sister. "Jody, they've taken Mother in an ambulance to Saint Martin's Hospital. I'll meet you there."

THEY SIT WAITING for the results as the doctor examines their mother.

"I bet it was those damn cigarettes," Jody complains.

Colleen shakes her head in agreement. "What are we going to do now?"

Jody shrugs. "I guess, just wait and see what happens."

"I hope she gets better."

Jody sets her hand on Colleen's. "I'm afraid it's too late. I bet she has lung cancer."

Colleen nods.

They sit in silence for a while. Then Jody looks over at Colleen. "I'm sorry for not listening to you about Eric Lau. It was insensitive of me. I shouldn't have been so hard on you."

"That's okay. You thought I was calling to whine about him. You didn't know." Colleen touches her sister's arm; she's forgiven her.

"No, it's not. If I did what you asked, you wouldn't have gone into hiding and ended up staying with that man."

"It wasn't so bad." Colleen tells her with a slight smile.

"I know you told Mother he was your boyfriend, but I don't believe it," Jody glares at her. "What were you doing with him, anyway? Weren't you scared? He was a stranger. He could have been a psychopath."

Colleen thinks of Jason. "At first, I wasn't sure what to expect. But the more I got to know him, the better I liked him. It sounds absurd, but I felt a genuine connection to him."

Jody shakes her head. "You always were weird."

"I know. I was born that way. Just look at my feet." Colleen smirks, but it fades fast. "I wanted to please Mother, but I wanted my freedom, too. I don't know why it bothers me so much to be away from the water, but it does. I know Mother worries about me a lot."

"She's obsessed with you. I was so jealous growing up. I

guess that's why I was always mean to you." Jody puts her arm around Colleen. "Can you forgive me?"

"I tried to fit in, but Mother wanted me to be more like you. You were the one she's most proud of," Colleen replies.

They hug, wiping away their tears.

———

COLLEEN PACES, occasionally looking out the large glass window of her high-rise condo at the view of Lake Union, with businesses and tall buildings surrounding the water as though it's their private pond. The boats on the lake below move about, traversing in the wind while dodging each other in the race they were having.

Colleen longs to be out on the open water near Cook's Cove. She slumps her shoulders. She's more a prisoner here in Seattle than she was with Jason. Other people built a cage around her—her bars are made of guilt. She can't leave; she owes it to her parents to stay.

Standing in the bathroom in front of the mirror, her reflection shows dark circles under her eyes. Logic tells her she isn't responsible for her mother's illness, but her disappearance contributed to it. Knowing her mother, she chain-smoked like a fiend during the days people were searching for her.

———

VISITING THE HOSPITAL, she finds her mother weak. Still, Alice insists on speaking. Colleen pulls up a chair and puts her ear close to her mother's mouth.

"I know you've been curious about where you came

from and who your parents are." She takes in a raspy breath, then waits a moment. "Next time you go to the house in Cook's Cove, there is something of yours in my bedroom. It's in the middle drawer. Inside, you will find a small piece of fur. It's a baby seal's skin."

"Shh, you need to rest your voice."

Her mother ignores her and keeps talking. "That fur was in the box when I found you on the water. It's the only thing that belonged to your birth mother. It's yours. You should keep it now."

Alice takes a breath, then continues, "For a long time, I thought you would run away if you knew about it. I wish I could tell you more, but I can't. The truth is…, I don't know who your mother is. She might've been a Native American teenager from the nearby reservation who didn't want a baby. No one knows. All I know is that she didn't want you, and I did."

Her mother stops, then swallows, her voice coming out as a whisper, "I'm sorry that I wasn't a better mother. I can see now that I should've let you be who you are rather than keep trying to change you. You need to follow your own path, not mine or your father's. To tell you the truth, I never wanted the business, either. I spent years trying to be someone I thought I was supposed to be, and I resented it. I guess I took it out on you, thinking that was what women did—shove their feelings down. It only made me miserable and angry all the time. I'm sorry. If you don't want to be involved in your father's business, you don't have to. You have my permission to sell your shares."

Colleen's eyes fill with tears. "Thank you." She kisses her mother's forehead.

Taken from the Sea

BETWEEN WORRYING about her mother's declining health and wondering about Jason, Colleen's exhausted. It's hard to maintain a cheerful disposition after spending several nights taking turns with Jody next to her mother's hospital bed, listening to her try to breathe through a tube. Alice is on morphine and barely conscious. It's as though her mother already died, and she's just keeping the ghost of a body company while it shuts down.

Sitting in her mother's room at Saint Martin's Hospital, Colleen stares up at the TV mounted on the wall. The news is on. The show teeters between news and entertainment by interjecting tidbits of gossip about local events. Most of which is made up of misconceptions and lies.

A photo of her and her mother taken years ago flashes on the screen.

"While Alice Monroe lies dying in her hospital bed, one wonders about the future of Monroe Shipping. Her daughter, Colleen, was recently found alive after missing for over two months. One wonders if Ms. Monroe's disappearance was a ploy to distract from the poor management decisions after Charles Monroe's death. Why else would Mr. Lei's sudden, mysterious departure to China prompt him to forfeit his shares in Monroe Shipping?

"As if this scandal isn't enough, we just learned that Eric Lau committed suicide in jail, leaving people to speculate why. According to a reliable source, Lau, an employee at Monroe Shipping and former boyfriend of Ms. Monroe, was recently arrested for his alleged role in a plot to kill his girlfriend. However, details and the motive remain a mystery. A lover's quarrel, perhaps? Rumor has it that Ms.

Monroe had a secret lover she was hiding with while presumed missing. However, this is pure speculation, as there is no evidence to support this."

So, Eric killed himself? There's no mention of the Triad or their plot to take over her father's business by killing her entire family. The government is keeping the information secret while they finish their investigation.

Chewing on her fingernail, she recalls Ben telling her he was successful at steering the police and the press away from Jason like he'd promised. Assuring them after his investigation that he found no evidence of any wrongdoing on Jason's part.

Colleen lets out a heavy sigh. This will be old news soon. She turns off the TV. Dread drifting over her like a full rain cloud needing a release. What is she to do now? She can't pick up the pieces from her past and snap them together again. Jody's the one with goals and schedules, not her. She needs to figure out a way forward in the world. Find a job somewhere that will keep her mind busy and off daydreams. She can't wander aimlessly forever. What's wrong with her? Why can't she be like everyone else and settle? Why is the water constantly calling to her?

━━

COLLEEN'S READING a sailing magazine when the heart monitor flatlines, and the buzzer goes off. A nurse rushes in. Colleen stands up and backs away. She's numb. The woman who raised her is now dead.

Colleen brings her hands to her face; it's finally over. Their struggle is over. She no longer has to follow her

Taken from the Sea

mother's wishes, and her mother no longer has to worry about her running into the water and disappearing.

Looking over at the pale body that has been guiding her life, she realizes that even though the woman isn't her birth mother, she never doubted her love.

Chapter Thirty

Colleen

Colleen powers her boat out of the marina, then turns off the engine. The sails rise like white wings, catching the wind, carrying her forward across the rippling sea. The sky is as open as the ocean before her, inviting her to come on its endless journey to that spiritual place in her heart.

When she reaches the island where the seals are, she drops her sails and anchor. Then, picking up her scuba gear and slipping it on, she goes to the side and jumps in, swimming over to the beach.

She removes her wetsuit and climbs up on a rock, claiming her space among the barking ladies. They are glad to see her. But soon, her joy turns to disappointment. She is comfortable around seals, but she feels like an outsider. Her heart sinks. She is a foreigner here, a tourist.

A tear mixes with salt, stinging her eyes. She reflects on

her life—how Alice gave her everything she thought a young girl would want.

Taking a deep breath, she looks out over the water. For her entire life, she has felt like an impostor hidden inside this body. A guest in her mother's world. If she never really belonged there, where does she belong?

Getting up, she dusts the sand from her legs. Strolling the beach, she spots a half-submerged chunk of wood stuck in the sand. Going to the piece, she pries it loose, then throws it in the water. The wood splashes, then bobs before the tide pushes the floating piece toward the shore again.

She was told she was found in a box floating near their house in Cook's Cove. Why did her birth mother abandon her? Does she have a family somewhere? Siblings who looked like her? Do they share her love of the water, too? Perhaps she'll never know.

A bark draws her attention, and she glances over to see three seals looking at her. She smiles. Were those animal spirits sent from another world to watch over her? Her water cousins?

She closes her eyes, letting the breeze rush past her. It's easy to believe anything out here, and it would appear real in her mind. She can imagine Jason's voice in the wind and sees him before her. They are dancing on the surface of the water under the smile of the moon.

Colleen wraps her arms around herself. He is holding her close to him. She can feel his heart beating in rhythm with her own. When she opens her eyes, she almost expects to find him in front of her. Realizing he isn't there, she picks up her stuff, slips on her suit and tank, then walks into the water and dives in.

As she turns her boat toward Cook's Cove, her heart

aches. She misses Jason. Is it wrong for her to have feelings for this man? She read about Stockholm Syndrome, but somehow it doesn't fit her experience. Jason never hurt her; he is a kind, gentle person. He's different from everyone else, just like she is.

She stares out at the water. A vision of his handsome face with those beautiful gray eyes makes her sigh. The image fades back behind his beard. Maybe he is the mystical creature, not her—someone who's stepped out of a folklore book and into her life. A prince disguised as a fisherman, laying his bounty at her feet. Her *webbed* feet.

IT'S STILL early in the afternoon. In the distance, a thin cloud of gray is moving east toward the marina. She lifts the strap of her bag containing her gear onto her shoulder and walks to her car.

Following the road to her parent's house, listening to the music on her radio, thoughts of Jason creep into her mind, and she wonders how he's doing. She impulsively drives past the entrance to her driveway. Traveling the highway, she thinks about where Jason's house is hiding along the road.

Spotting the 'Do Not Enter' sign, she slams on the brakes, almost missing the turn. Entering the driveway, she passes a 'No Trespassing' sign. As she gets closer, she recognizes the surrounding area—the tall evergreen trees and the water below. Parking next to his rusty old truck, she gets out, running to the front of his house, then knocking loudly on the door. When he doesn't answer, she realizes he isn't inside and goes to the dock. His boat's gone.

Taken from the Sea

She squints, searching the horizon, but doesn't find his boat. In the distance, a patch of gray hovering above the water is growing larger, gobbling up more of the sky.

After waiting an hour, she goes to the shed. A padlock hangs from the door. Should she leave or wait in her car? The air's cool, and she senses rain coming, so she grabs her coat from the back seat and puts it on.

Colleen walks to the beach to wait. Five minutes grows into an hour. The sun is shutting down for the night, and the evening is setting up its watch over the water. *Why am I here? Maybe this was a mistake, and I should just leave. He'd never know I came looking for him.*

Thunder rumbles. Grasping the front of her coat, she pulls the collar up to protect her neck from the chilly air.

In the distance, a beam of light bounces, and a boom explodes around her. Flashes crack the blue marble sky into pieces. The rain comes down on the dirt. She runs to the edge of the dock. A slight glow of light is heading in her direction.

The heavens split open, and a downpour drenches her, parting dark strands of hair that fall along her face. When the boat approaches the dock, she waves. Jason throws the rope, which she quickly grabs and secures. He climbs the steps, a new cane at his side. He pulls back his hood.

She wipes the rain from her eyes. The light from the post lights his image, and she can see a shadow of a beard on his face. His hair's outgrown its cut and is now shaggy.

"What do you want?" he asks abruptly.

It's not the reaction she is hoping for.

"I wanted to see you."

The sky flashes again.

"You picked a hell of a time for that." He whines a rope around his arm and elbow.

The sky grumbles and throws more rain at them.

She wipes the water running down her face. "Maybe we can go inside and talk?"

"I've got work to do. A catch to unload." He sets the coiled rope down.

"I can help," Colleen says, walking toward him. "Let me help you. Please."

Jason stands for a moment, then slowly steps to where she is, throwing off his gloves, dropping his cane, taking her in his arms. When he kisses her, her knees buckle. She raises her arms and places them around his neck. The water runs down the top of their heads as they continue kissing. The feel of his lips sweeps her away. She wants nothing more than to be with him.

"Oh Selkie," he whispers when he stops kissing her. He takes her hand, leading her over to the door of his house. "I'll tend to my catch later," he says, unlocking it.

Inside, he sheds his wet coat and rubber overalls, leaving them in a pile on the tile floor in the entryway. Now in his long underwear, he helps her out of her coat and clothes, pulling her T-shirt over her head, unfastening her bra, and sliding her pants down. His touch is fire on her skin. He scoops her up, carrying her down the hall with a limp. He kicks the door to his bedroom wide open and places her on the bed. Then he strips and crawls beside her.

She gasps at the feel of his lips as they travel up and down, kissing every part of her body. It lights up with feelings she never experienced before. She wants him. All of him. She smiles when he looks down at her, and a grin spreads across his face. An explosion of pleasure shoots through her, and she calls out his name, "Jason." Together, they merge into one, as natural as the incoming tide.

IN THE MORNING, he brings her a cup of coffee in bed and sits next to her on the mattress in his T-shirt and boxers. He runs his hand up and down her arm gently.

"Why did you come here, Selkie—I mean, Colleen?"

She feels the pull of energy in his touch, then notices the rock in the shape of a heart she gave him on the table. "I think this is where I belong." She takes a sip, then sets the cup down.

"Here?" He stops and tilts his head. His gray eyes holding hers.

"Yes, with you." She reaches out and touches his face, feeling the growth of his sprouting beard.

He takes her hand and kisses the palm.

"I want to be with you." She smiles. "I want to sail around the world with you. I want to be your wife if you'll have me."

He runs his hand down the side of her head. A smile forms in his mouth. "Ah, Selkie. You'd make me the happiest man in the world. But I have nothing to offer you. You should go back to your rich family so you can live like a princess."

"Jason, I have plenty of money of my own. I've sold my interest in Monroe Shipping. I don't have anything keeping me away now. My sister doesn't want me hanging around her. The woman who raised me just died of cancer. So, you see, I have no one to go back to."

He kisses her knuckles. "So, you'd rather be with me, a

fisherman, then with some other fella, living in some fancy place in the city?"

"Yes, Jason. I love you."

He stares at her for a moment, taking in what she just said. He draws her close to him. She rests her head on his chest, and he kisses the top of her hair.

"After that day in the hospital, I was afraid I'd never see you again. My life has been so empty without you. I don't want to ever lose you." He hugs her tightly. "I love you so much. I'll do whatever it takes to make you happy."

She pulls back and looks at him. "Just be yourself, Jason. I love you just the way you are."

Epilogue

There are mysteries all around Cook's Cove that no one can explain. The truth lies somewhere between the twilight of dreams and the stories we tell ourselves about what things mean. Spirits searching for new places to inhabit often appear and disappear, making the impossible possible. So, one shouldn't be surprised by the desire to know the story behind that bit of fur and the baby in the box. Unfortunately, Alice Monroe only realized upon her death what she knew in her heart was true all along. That happens when you die sometimes, just before your spirit flies off.

The seals often watched Alice as she walked along the sand. They knew she wanted a child, and one of theirs wished to return to her family in the ocean.

Earlier that morning, the wind silenced the screams. The other ladies followed along like shadows in the water, waiting patiently. Finally, the baby broke through and was born in the bottom of a canoe from a mother with webbed feet. The child's mother was their sister, who was captured farther north years before. Only recently, she found her skin and left behind the fisherman who caught her. But she was heavy with child. Wanting to break all ties with the human world, she made a sacrifice.

The tide pushed the canoe closer to shore. She placed the infant in the wooden box, along with a piece of fur. Her half-selkie child would be better in a world of humans. It couldn't survive in the world her mother had come from.

She kissed her infant goodbye, then slipped into her skin. The bottom of the canoe was pierced. Water flowed in, covering the evidence as it sank. She crawled out of the canoe, sending the box closer to the shore. Once she saw Alice on the beach, she dove into the sea to return home with the other seals, knowing her child was safe.

Perhaps Colleen would never learn the truth as to why the water called to her, for she had fallen in love with the man who captured her. They would sail across the ocean, gliding above the water, where they would live out their own myth as the selkie and the fisherman.

IF YOU ENJOYED this book please leave a review. You opinion is important. Readers read reviews. It helps them to decide if this story is something they would like to read. Thank you.

To learn about other books by Judy Leslie and to sign up for behind the scenes info and free goodies go to her website:

Judy-leslie.com

Acknowledgments

I would like to thank my husband Ralph and my friends for their support. Especially the ladies in my book club for not getting upset with me when I haven't read the month's book. A special thanks goes to the editors that have helped make my stories better and my cover designer for her wonderful designs.

My house hasn't been as tidy and my meals haven't been fancy while I've been sitting at my computer dreaming up stories. But my family understands in order to create it takes time. I am thankful for everyone's support and understanding. Love you all!

Judy Leslie

About the Author

Who doesn't love a mystery? Throw in a bit of suspense and a romance and you're off on an adventure. Nothing like curling up with a good book on a rainy day or before you drop off to bed at night. Especially if there is a little strange activity lurking in the background.

The best way to describe her Cook's Cove collection is that they are mysteries with a romance containing emotional elements found in woman's fiction. Several of these stories lean towards the sweet with heat romance rather than spicy, but they also contain some darker elements.

Judy Leslie lives in the Pacific Northwest and splits her time between living in a city on the water and a cabin in the mountains.

She also writes contemporary small town romances that take place in the mountain town of Leavenworth, Washington. Visit her website for more info about upcoming books www.judy-leslie.com

Made in the USA
Monee, IL
12 July 2025

21015544R00128